Billy Keane is a sports columnist with the *Irish Independent* and runs the world-famous John B. Keane's pub in Listowel in his native County Kerry. His previous books include the novel *The Last of the Heroes, Rebel, Rebel: The Billy Morgan Story* (with Billy Morgan) and *Rucks, Mauls and Gaelic Football* (with Moss Keane).

First published in 2013 by
Liberties Press
140 Terenure Road North | Terenure | Dublin 6W
Tel: +353 (1) 405 5703
www.libertiespress.com | info@libertiespress.com

Trade enquiries to Gill & Macmillan Distribution
Hume Avenue | Park West | Dublin 12
T: +353 (1) 500 9534 | F: +353 (1) 500 9595 | E: sales@gillmacmillan.ie

Distributed in the UK by
Turnaround Publisher Services
Unit 3 | Olympia Trading Estate | Coburg Road | London N22 6TZ
T: +44 (0) 20 8829 3000 | E: orders@turnaround-uk.com

Distributed in the United States by
Dufour Editions | PO Box 7 | Chester Springs | Pennsylvania | 19425

Copyright © Billy Keane, 2013
The author has asserted his moral rights.

ISBN: 978-1-907593-97-0
2 4 6 8 10 9 7 5 3 1

A CIP record for this title is available from the British Library.

Cover design by Anna Morrison
Internal design by Liberties Press

The publishers gratefully acknowledge financial assistance from the Arts Council.

The
Ballad
of
Mo & G

Billy Keane

LIB
ERT
IES

For Tim O'Carroll

The owners of dogs related to wolves always say, 'Ah Fido. Ah but my poor old Fido wouldn't harm a fly.'

Well dogs don't eat flies, do they? Unless they swallow one by accident.

The Olsen hounds stalked the Compound. All day and all night. Silently, on soft pads.

Mo imagined the dogs were keeping her under house arrest, like a political prisoner.

Even though I wished it was me she was married to, I was still hoping Mo would be happy ever after with Dermo Olsen. That was until the violence started.

I loved her that much.

Can you believe that?

The Olsen family kept their fighting dogs in a secret concentration camp.

At the far end of the Olsen land. Well in from the road, in a dip, hidden by ivy-strangled trees and a doodle of climbing thorn bushes.

We wandered down to the fortress when the guard dogs were at the vet for shots. That morning Dermo kissed Mo goodbye and told her he was off to Wales on a driving job, in his big lorry.

The eight-strong litter of Doberman pups were playing behind strands of barbed wire attached to concrete posts. A saggy brood bitch with a mangy coat, as well worn as the dole office mat, sat in the centre of the circle.

Her puppies were climbing and falling off a dead donkey with the glassiest, saddest eyes you ever saw. The manic babies tore at the tattered flesh of the sinewy ass. Every now and then the pups broke off from the donkey and jumped up at a rabbit hanging by the neck from a sycamore branch. The rabbit was suspended just a few centimetres over the pups' maximum reach. The Dobermans were leppin' up, trying to snatch at the meat they could never quite reach. Two and three would jump together, like footballers contesting a high ball.

The rabbit hardly took his own life.

It must have been Dermo.

He must have been the one who hanged Bugs Bunny.

Stripped carcasses, old bleached bones and fresh dog dirt were scattered all over the filthy run. I was barely able to breathe and Mo, who was suffering from morning sickness, threw up. We left the runs but the stink followed us up the hill.

Then, as we reached the second grove of trees, about half-way up, there was a revved-up chain saw noise.

We listened for a few seconds, without moving. It was Dermo. He was driving fast across the fields, hopping and bumping on his quad bike, as he hit every bump and hollow.

We hid ourselves further into the trees.

Dermo pulled up suddenly outside the runs. The bike skidded round and back in the direction in which it was coming from, leaving a track in the mud in the shape of a semicolon. It was as if he was showing off in front of the Dobermans.

Dermo grabbed the small dog by the back of the neck from a cardboard box. He dipped the little dog in a bucket of blood. It was a Papillon, a butterfly dog. With long, limp ears and short legs. Red dripped and mixed with the cow-brown patches on his white coat. The Papi barked and barked.

We didn't intervene in any way. Well we couldn't, could we? It happened so quickly, we didn't have time.

Dermo threw the little Papi over the high wire and into

the Dobermans' den. The flying butterfly dog,with his clown's ears flapping and his chicken legs kicking, tried to pedal his way upwards on an invisible bike. Gravity kicked in.

The mother sprung to life. She intercepted the Papi just before it hit the ground. The dog screamed. It was a human sound of absolute terror. Then the pups attacked when the mother casually dropped the convulsing Papi and walked away towards a stainless steel water bowl. She took a drink and then looked back at her pupils.

The small dog was torn asunder like a Christmas cracker, with one of the killers pulling from the head end and the other from the tail.

We couldn't watch anymore.

As we moved quickly through the trees and down the other side of the hill in the direction of the Compound, we could hear Coach Dermo shout, 'Drink him, drink him. Ye little vampires, ye.'

His loud, amplified laughter echoed from the old fort as it chased us into a run.

'Ate him, lads. Go on boys, ate him. Go on. Ate him up.'

Dermo's roaring followed us up and over the hill like a cloud of poisonous gas. The Dobermans were barking in a nonstop frenzy. We stopped when we were well out of sight of the runs on the far side of the hill.

'How did I end up with him? How, G? Jesus, G. How?'

Mo sat on her heels as she rocked back and forth with her hands on either side of her head.

I knelt beside her and put my arms around her.

We both knew the answer.

It wasn't as if Mo fell in love.

Dermo made Mo pregnant.

His foreplay was a case of lager.

She too was very drunk on the night they made the baby.

Deliberately so on her part.

It was the way.

I can only do it when I'm pissed.

Barriers fell before the flood of booze.

She could hardly remember.

Up against the wall.

Somehow it was in her head she should be doing it.

Like as in I'm twenty-two.

I should be having sex.

Everyone is.

And what is it anyway?

What's it to anyone?

When it's over, it's over.

'It took 2.2 minutes approx.'

A man who polished his zips with Brasso would have to be quick.

'It wasn't the best shag ever,' Mo said, 'but it was definitely the fastest.'

No condom.

Forgot to buy a pack in the shop.

Machine broken in the club, as usual.

'I'll pull out,' he promised.

He didn't hold her.

Zipped up his shiny zip and fucked off.

The morning-after pill was taken two mornings after.

And it failed.

In the beginning, Mo liked the idea of living in the Olsen Compound.

She figured if it's a Compound, it must be safe and agreed to move in without a preview.

Mo was three months pregnant and she had nowhere else to go.

It would never change, she thought. Whatever way you looked at it, no matter how many times she twisted it around in her head, Mo would forever be halves in a baby with Dermo Olsen. Even if they split up, he would still have rights over their kid. And Mo, who never really had a dad, thought she should at least try to make a go of it.

As Mo saw it, back then, an accidental father is better than no father at all.

In the run-up to the wedding, he hardly uttered a word. Mo interpreted this as a sign Dermo was the strong, silent type. The way I see it is, Mo tried to fit Dermo into a category before she ever really got to know him.

The Olsens encouraged the marriage. They had their own strict code; if you made a girl pregnant, you married her. It was their way. Olsens would grow up Olsens and there was no letting go.

Mo was shocked when she saw the Compound as it really was.

Half-stripped cars were broken up all over the muddy yard like a bombed convoy. Three green and gold Olsen Transport lorry cabs genuflected. Tied to the side of a rusty padlocked shed was a large hardboard sign, 'Trespassers Will Be Ate'. The potholes in the junkyard were deep enough to bathe a baby in.

The half-Alsatian, half-greyhound mongrel named Grey licked his privates. An old broken-windowed bus that once took pensioners to bingo at night, and children to school the next morning, was a dog dormitory, where ogres of hounds slept with one eye open.

And the stink was everywhere.

It wouldn't have been too bad if Mo lived in a housing estate with neighbours to pass the time with, but only Olsens lived near Olsens.

The first house on the left, just past the heart of the junkyard, was owned by Dermo's mother, Maureen. Mikey Olsen, Dermo's older brother, lived in the third bungalow. Mo was in the middle.

There was no privacy. Olsens wandered in and out without ever knocking.

Mo and Dermo were in the shower making love. Sorry, 'having sex,' as Mo put it. Mo liked sex, a lot.

Maureen pounded furiously at the bathroom door. 'Who's in there?' she demanded in her always hoarse, forty-a-day voice.

'Just us, Mammy!' shouted Dermo.

THE BALLAD OF MO & G

'Get out of there pronto. And I mean pronto . . . Right now.'

There was no taking on Maureen. She was as big as a Sumo's mammy and even the Olsens were scared of her.

Ma Olsen wore gold hula-hoops on her ears. My old man used to say never mess with a woman if your fist fits through her earrings.

She banged on the door again. Louder this time.

Mo found a few clothes pegs on a bathroom shelf and fastened a makeshift bra from towels. The way her mother-in-law was carrying on, Mo was sure the house was on fire. She panicked and ran into the bedroom.

'What were yez doing in there?' demanded Ma Olsen.

Mo was fumbling with towels.

'Sparin' the hot water, Mammy?' replied Dermo, who was wearing a non-slip rubber bathroom mat as a toga.

Mo's improvised bra-towel slipped a little, momentarily.

Her mother-in-law was still angry her Dermo had to marry someone he hardly knew. The first time she met Mo was two days before the wedding.

'You have small boobs for feeding a child. He'll starve if he's dependin' on dem,' remarked Maureen Olsen, who, like all mothers-in-law, everywhere, without exception, without a frigging millidoubt, in my opinion, greatly resented any woman having sex with her son.

Even though they wouldn't hand back the resultant babies, Oedipus was the controlling complex.

Which of course has being going on for thousands of years and must definitely be a true hypothesis as the Greeks knew only too well in those plays they wrote, back in the days when they had brains.

When Mo complained to Dermo for not sticking up for her, his only remark was, 'Who the fuck is pronto?'

Ma Olsen must have been jealous.

Once on the Luas, at rush hour, when the packed tram stopped suddenly, I touched Mo's boobs by accident. Mo had beautiful breasts. Mo didn't seem to make any effort to fold her arms but maybe she didn't have time.

Sometimes if she bent downwards, I could see the hard fabricated rim of her bra which was usually only half a bra or a half-cup, as the celebrity chefs say on TV when they tell us how much hummus to put in some hippy shit no one ever bothers to cook.

I am pretty sure she never saw me looking.

Sure enough. And sure enough too, it was an accident on the Luas. But you would be sort of hoping. They say you always know when they fancy you and that women have their signs and hints.

We were not lovers. Which is pretty obvious, if I didn't actually get to feel her breasts, other than at near disasters on Titanic trams. There was a tacit acceptance that if I made a move, it might ruin the friendship. Well that was how I saw it and I did give Mo some thought and some more thought after that.

We sort of loved each other. Well I love her and would definitely make love to her but she would have to ask me.

It was more than friendship. I know that much.

I know too, for sure, Mo would never kill me.

Mo confronted Dermo, even though I warned her to keep quiet about the slaughter of the little Papi.

Mo, being Mo, couldn't let the cruelty go. Possibly she was trying to change him. That this was part of her grand plan to de-dog Dermo.

Mo stood arms folded and legs slightly apart as Dermo tried to explain himself.

'I was only trainin' dem ickle Dobermen for guarding things. From knackers and dudder robbers what has no consciences. Gets 'em good, and vicious, Babe. Foreplay for fuckin' fightin' to the death. Do you know what I mane? They gotta get blooded. Don't they? There's bettin' goin' on at the fight nights. What do you think pays for the dogs? Their children's allowances, is it?'

Dermo argued the Papi was 'already dead anyways and was road kill, a dumped orphan what didn't get no rosette in the gay dog show. It's the same's a dead man donatin' his organs.'

Mo laughed a bitter laugh and shouted right in his face, 'You're a ventriloquist then. A dog ventriloquist. What about the barking? I didn't know dead dogs barked. And don't call me Babe. I'm not your Babe. I'm your bitch.'

Her loving husband didn't like sarcasm very much.

Dermo turned away as if he was choosing to ignore her.

He swung round unexpectedly and slapped her with the knuckles of his left hand, loosening one of her front teeth. Mo had perfect teeth. She brushed and flossed every day, even when she was a small girl.

Mo made for Dermo and hit him with her closed fist. The force of the blow was no more than a fly landing on an elephant.

Dermo kicked her away from him, in the stomach, with his steel reinforced work boot.

The sole left a muddy herring bone footprint on her bulging white top. As if he walked over her for a shortcut. Dermo left Mo bent on the floor, in the foetal position, and on the way out he slammed the door so hard the glass cracked.

Later that night Mo was taken to the hospital. She was bleeding from the uterus.

That was the night she lost her baby.

I called to see Mo in St Hilda's.

Mo's lips were bruised. She moved her loose tooth back and forth with her index finger, like a cat flap.

'It's going to fall out, G. I'm going to have to put a false tooth soaking in a glass to clean off the plaque. Like my Ma.'

The baby had to be vacuumed out of her, she said, but it was all very matter of fact, which was really worrying. The nurses and the doctors wanted to call the Gardaí but Mo was afraid to tell them anything. The excuse was she was playing football and a stray shot hit her accidentally in the tummy.

'You have to leave him,' was my advice.

Mo turned away.

'I have nowhere to go.'

'Your mother? Get a Ryanair over. Stay until you get sorted.'

Mo sighed with frustration. I went round to the other side of the bed so I could see her face.

'Let me spell it out for you, G. My mother is in England.

She has a man. Bob Five Bellies is his name. They spend all day smoking dope and eating oven chips. Bob claims to be a talent scout for dancers. But he's really a driver for blonde girls who dance on fat men's bellies. Got that?'

Sometimes the words come out before you have time to stop them.

'Is she sort of a hooker's chaperone then? Your Mam?'

'She's hooker lite. It's really nice that, for both sides. Bob's mates think they've pulled. They give Ma a little present. Ma thinks the men love her so much and that she's not really on the game.'

Mo never knew her old man. Her Dad vamoosed one day when he won money at the bookies, not long after Mo was born, and died from the booze and dope when she was five or six.

'Ah never mind your mother. Surely you're not going back to Dermo. That nutter could kill you.'

I was now finished forever with wishing well on the marriage.

Mo pulled herself up. Grimaced as she held the metal protectors on the side of the bed

'I have nowhere to go. I told you. For now.'

I wrote out a cheque behind a screen where life was so often altered or ended, and people in a bad way had to whisper last words of love and goodbye.

'That will fix your tooth. The orthodontist can put in a permanent implant and nobody will know anything or notice it's not real.'

In a temper, she whooshed away the cheque off the mobile table straddling the bed. It flew like a paper plane under the screen separating us from the other patients in the maternity ward.

Mothers were nursing babies and more were on drips. In the background the hospital's own radio station played oldies songs to make sick people sicker. A baby cried and another joined in.

Mo cried nearly every time she heard a baby cry.

I picked up the cheque and folded it neatly. So as to make it seem smaller.

'Please take it.'

And she did. Mo sat up and opened out the cheque

'It's a loan. Ah thanks, G. It's kinda cute what with your name signed on it. Like your autograph. You had it written out. Thanks, G. You really are my best friend.'

She smiled at me but with her mouth closed.

'Hey, G,' she said, perking up at the thought of the good old days.

'Do you remember the night in Angel Lane? '

It was a mad college party. Nearly five years ago. In a heaving club. The place was lifting. I had to shout the chat-up lines at Mo above the mad music.

'Remember when we were young the way it was how the mother always gave us Dozo. When we were sick? For fevers and stuff?'

Mo bent down to my height.

'Go on. I hear you.'

I made my pitch.

'I'm making a new drink from baby dope and booze. *DoZoPop* it's gonna be called. It'll be like drinking in the womb. I'm gonna be rich.'

Mo was studying Business and I was in First Year Civil

Engineering. Mo warned me she was from a part of the city that was always in the news for drugs and gangs murdering each other.

'But you don't have a really strong accent? You spoofin' me?' I asked. Mo took of her heels. Now we were almost the same height.

Mo told me she spent 'three long years in the poshest boarding school in the country. On scholarship.'

Her friend came back with two off-duty cops.

Mo's pal hitched herself up. 'Me knickers is riding me.'

'Come on,' said one of the cops. 'I'm on at six.'

'Sorry, G, I gotta look after her. She's pissed. You know how it is.'

I tailed the girls. Secretly. By the exit, the bigger of the two policeman grabbed Mo's arse and she didn't take any notice.

Her friend said, referring to me, 'I wouldn't ride that little runt if he had pedals.'

We met in college the very next day. After a while I stopped trying to impress Mo and I was myself.

Told Mo my Dad was very sick.

Told her, 'Dad lost a leg.' How it was he put an ad in *Buy and Sell* magazine: 'For Sale 7 left shoes.' I hadn't told anyone about the ad. I didn't want people who didn't really know Dad to think he was crazy. But Mo laughed like mad and said my Dad must be a gas man. She promised to pray for him in the college chapel.

I was well in love with her by then.

We met up most days after that.

The lady who had the hysterectomy on the other side of a plastic screen with dolphins swimming in every direction broke the recall when she pressed long on her buzzer for another room-service painkiller.

A smiling man holding a bouquet of red roses opened Mo's curtains and apologised.

'I thought he was bringing me a wreath for my dead baby.'

What could I say to that?

I was so deadly scared of Dermo.

We could have gone anywhere with my civil engineering qualifications. But I just couldn't ask her. There was always the worry that if I told her how I felt, she would dump me as a friend. I just didn't know how to close the deal.

Mo was a beautiful looking girl. Taller than me. Black, silky, Spanish hair, and a body that was designed by the lads who made mannequins for shop windows. Her big brown eyes were a deeper brown than my mother's mahogany hall table and her lips always seemed moist and full. That's when they weren't slapped multicoloured by Dermo.

I should have taken the plunge there and then.

I knew for sure Dermo would come after us. Every day there was a murder on the news. The Olsens probably knew hit men. But Dermo would hardly sub-contract a job he would enjoy doing so much himself.

He was capable of castration. Put my testicles in my shoes. I think that was what the Mafia did if you ran away with one of their wives. The tradition was kept in hick villages in Sicily or in Little Italy in New York until the net was invented. Now crazies everywhere have a guide.

'Sleep on it. I'll call back tomorrow.'

I kissed her on the top of the head. She didn't seem to notice that this was the first time I ever actually kissed her anywhere.

'Hey, G?' she asked, as if trying to get out of the here and now. 'Do you remember what you said to me when I asked you in the club . . . the first night . . . if the horrible orange dress was awful on me?'

I did remember, but Mo answered her own question.

'You said I would look good in an onion bag.'

Mo changed mood again.

'I told Dermo I wished he was dead and I do,' she said quietly.

'The world takes revenge on people like him. There's no need to go to the cops, if you think about it. Bad things happen to bad people. Karma's just another word for dues. He will die soon.'

The attack took place in the supermarket queue, just a few days before Mo lost her little baby.

Mo emptied her shopping on the rolling conveyor belt.

Mrs D dramatically banged the yellow supermarket partition between her dog food and Mo's shopping. There were fifteen tins of Fido beef with onion gravy on Mrs D's territory, even though she didn't own a dog.

Mrs D probably made burgers and lasagne from the Fido.

Mrs D put her arms around Mo's big bump and squeezed as tight as she could. Mo released Mrs D's interlocked witch's wrists with difficulty. Then Mrs D opened fire.

'You're a slut robber like your whore mother. Look at your black pudding fingers with your mock pound shop ring. Fat fingers, fat fingers, fat fingers, fat fingers,' she called out like cruel school yards kids do, in a sing-song voice.

As bad luck would have it, a Taiwanese machine for sucking up leaves was on special offer and there were loads of people in the supermarket to snap up the bargain. It was late May and there were no fallen leaves on the ground. There wasn't much point in sucking live leaves off trees in May. Unless you're a giraffe that is.

That was the way it was back in the boom.

Mrs D went at it non-stop. Told Mo she was a nobody and her mother was a ride who rode Mr D loads of times.

It was the first time Mo had heard of her mother's alleged affair with Mr D.

Mo wanted to get out of the shop but she couldn't find her purse in the large cluttered bag. A young mother with a baby tied to her front, said 'Let me try.' She put her hand deep into Mo's bag and pulled out the purse.

'Lucky dip,' she said in a caring voice.

Her baby's knitted hat had fallen into Mo's bag.

Mo bent over to retrieve the baby bonnet.

'That's how she takes it!' screamed Mrs D. ' Like a dog. Look at her. Look at her. Woof woof, woof woof.' And then she began to pant with her long, off-white, waxy tongue flapping out of the side of her mouth.

Heads turned down faraway isles. Shoppers left whatever it was they were examining. A thin man looking at a money-saving device for cutting his own hair walked hurriedly towards the checkout. He fumbled for his iPhone.

Mo put her hands up to her face to avoid the shower of spitty spray. And to hide her face from the thin iPhone man, who was only a few metres away filming like frigging Spielberg. The director put most of the rant up on YouTube for all the world to see. Without Mo's okay. It's there forever now. Mo was worried the movie might go viral. And would strangers point to her in the street and say 'Look, there's the lady in the mad dog food fight on YouTube.'

Mo felt vulnerable, now that she was so far gone.

Running through her head was the scary thought Mrs D might damage her baby.

Mrs D kicked over a column of aromatherapy foot spas. The top spa fell on her head. A bottle of jasmine oil broke open but the scent failed to calm Mrs D.

She screamed.

'I hope your bastard baby dies!'

The Polish checkout lady pushed Mrs D roughly out through the front of the shop.

Mrs D called for the police.

Mo almost collapsed. She leant over the Perspex protecting the cash register. Her sweating hands left the perfect imprint of a palm and fingers.

The Polish checkout lady was very nice to Mo. The girl with the baby said 'Take no notice of her, she's off the head. Here take a drink of water.' Mo swallowed most of the small bottle in one go.

The shoppers went back to their juicers, German sauerkraut and satellites for tents. The girl with the baby stayed. Mo asked to go to the toilets.

Mrs D, who had doubled back into the shop, dodged from shelf to shelf for cover. She followed Mo to the staff toilets. Mo didn't lock the cubicle. Mrs D pushed her face into Mo's.

Mo pulled back from the stench of dog breath. There was no escape. Mo was trapped. She folded her arms round her bump. This time Mrs D spoke slowly and deliberately, just above a whisper, but loud enough for Mo to hear every word.

'Your baby will be stillborn and they'll throw it in the

furnace. It'll burn like it was in hell cos of your whore mother.'

Mo sobbed. 'I hope you die. I hope you die soon.'

That was the moment.

The beginning of the wish-killing.

Mrs D was brought to the hospital by ambulance. She was gasping and wheezing. Mo was told by the supermarket people, who were tipped-off by the police. She was diagnosed with lung cancer, even though the woman never smoked a cigarette in her life.

Mrs D was 'opened and closed' according to the manager of the supermarket. 'She's a gonner,' he said, in a good-enough-for-her sort of voice.

Mo and Mrs D were in St Hilda's at the same time. Mo asked me to check on Mrs D, who was upstairs in the ward for lost causes.

The sign on the door of the intensive care unit read, 'Family members only'.

I pretended I was Mrs D's nephew Fintan. The name has such a ring of truth to it. A Fintan could never be suspected of telling lies.

Mrs D was attached to a drip feeding liquids in, and another pipe took liquids out. Two forked, stem-thin tubes were stuck up Mrs D's nostrils. Her moustache was as if he wiped her nose with a finger dipped in coal dust. Which made Mrs D into a grotesque, gasping walrus.

She didn't have enough breath to generate speech.

'This is your nephew Fintan,' announced the nurse, who was delighted Mrs D had a visitor.

Mrs D's pupils rolled around in her marzipan eyes. Her chest heaved and fell but didn't rise again. Spittle blobs formed on the corners of her mouth, but no words came out. A vein on the side of Mrs D's head turned purple as a slug. Mrs D tried to sit up but fell back.

And Fintan slipped away while the nurse was attending to Mrs D.

I reported back within a few minutes. Told Mo Mrs D was panting like a fish on the riverbank.

Mo sat up in the bed. 'She's mad. Off her game but I'm not sorry for her. I can try but I'm not sorry for her. It was an awful thing to say and her wish came true.'

We changed the subject. Spoke about job prospects and the chances of Mo going back to college.

'Hey, G. Be honest with me. Are my fingers fat?'

I had the line ready ever since I heard of Mrs D's attack.

'Mo you have the slender fingers of a piano player.'

She moved her hand slowly over mine.

'You should write poetry,' she said.

Mrs D died the very next day.

The police told the supermarket she died from shortage of breath. So Mo could hardly be charged with murder. Everyone dies from shortage of breath in the end. Well nobody ever died from some terminal disease and kept on breathing. Did they?

But Maureen was certain Mo had wish-killed Mrs D. That's Maureen, as in Dermo's mother. She was very worried for her son. Worried sick he would die in the near future from one of the several I-wish-he-was-deads made by Mo.

Maureen loved her precious book. She minded it like an old manuscript illuminated by the monks.

'It's my bible,' said Maureen.

Her hardback, dust covered, *The Law of the Wish* was without dog ears or thumb smears.

When Maureen was reading it, on went the surgical gloves. Sometimes if Maureen ran out of gloves, she went on her knees to blow open a new page. It often took her a whole day to read just two pages. Every sentence was checked and rechecked, several times, for new meanings. She asked Mo a thousand interpretation questions. And there were long phone calls to other Wishers.

Maureen joined up the Law of The Wish Foundation at the second highest level of associate membership. The book 'sold more copies than the bible' and the foundation had 23.3 million members.'Worldwide,' Maureen emphasised as if Mo thought the 23.3 were all living in Ireland, which wouldn't leave very much room for the rest of us.

There's more than one strand to *The Law of the Wish* but in the context of the alleged killing of Mrs D, it goes something like: if you wish someone the worst, and you are one of those with the power of life and death, the wishee is as good as dead.

Maureen was certain her son Dermo was doomed. After all, Mo did put a curse on him and now she was a proven killer. Maureen called next door to see Mo on the night she came home from the hospital. Dermo was on his way to the pub.

'Sorry bout dudder night,' he said before he left. 'Here's somethin' for you to get somethin' with. I shunta kicked you in the gee. I'm a sorry bout the babby, but he wadn't really a babby cos he wadn't rightly made inta a babby. But you shouldn't have gone knocking no dogs nader. There was no call for that. The dogs can't stand up for theirselves. They're dumb you know.'

Mo let go at Dermo.

'You prefer Doberman pups to babies. I will never forgive you, ever, you murderer. I wish you were dead.'

'Fuck you.' He snatched back the fifty. The note tore in two. Afraid now, she handed him the other half, at the same time watching his free hand.

Dermo banged the door so hard that the euro store porcelain duckling I bought for Mo as a take-the-piss wedding present smashed into smithereens on the floor.

Every time that man closed a door something broke.

That night, Maureen made Mo a stuffed chicken dinner with creamy mash and buttered carrots. Mo's mother-in-law made lovely dinners, with homemade gravy.

Indoors, Maureen always wore fluffy pink slippers in the shape of big bunnies. The slippers were covered with plastic bags to keep the rabbits clean and dry.

There was a new pair of matching bunny slippers for Mo 'to keep her toes warm.' And a block of ice cream with two packets of wafers.

'It's Cosmopolitan,' announced Maureen. 'Your favourite.'

After the dinner and the ice cream and the coffee, there was small talk. Then after only a few minutes, Maureen, who couldn't ever restrain herself if something was bothering her, asked Mo if she really meant her death wish for Dermo.

Mo didn't answer.

Maureen responded by trawling her calloused hands through her wild, variegated hair.

'I must get me roots done.'

Maureen took off her gold charm bracelet.

She twisted the tiny handle of the gold wishing well with her plump fingers.

'Seeing as I have no daughter of my own, I want this to

be yours when I'm gone. Please don't go murderin' our Dermo. I know what he done was terrible. I was dying for a little grandchild.'

Maureen began to cry. Mo put her arm around Maureen. It only went as far as the tip of the opposite shoulder blade.

'It's no bed of roses being an Olsen. I had it tough, but back in the old days I couldn't go nowhere. There was the kids and I had the lard walloped out me a good few times. I think that's why I got so fat. I ate to forget.'

'It's usually drink to forget,' replied Mo

She poured Maureen a top-up glass of Chateau Tuesday and the two watched TV. Maureen had a 52-inch TV installed for Mo when she was in the hospital and had all the channels put in.

'Paid for by our Dermo. In a shop.'

The TV programme was about the winning garden at the Chelsea flower show.

Maureen scraped the last of the melted ice cream off the cardboard carton with a knife and licked it clean. A yellow banana blob fell on the fluffy bunny.

'Look Maureen, the bunny's wearing fake tan.'

If there were ten cartons, Maureen would have eaten every one, for comfort's sake. Mo joked Maureen would even have eaten the fluffy bunny now there was ice cream on it. Maureen laughed and then she went all serious.

'Dermo kicked out at the table in a temper, but he missed. He was frustrated and upsetted. That's all. He didn't mean to hurt nobody. It was an accident. Our Dermo is no saint but he'd never kill a little babby.'

Mo didn't respond.

They watched a programme about celebrity chefs and celeriac. When it was over Maureen said, 'Careful what you wish for.'

'I am very careful,' replied Mo.

She knew that would upset Maureen but somehow she knew too that her mother-in-law would take heed and in turn would get to Dermo. Even mad sons listen to their mammies.

'Can you take back what you wished about Dermo dying?'

Mo looked at her mother-in-law full on.

'Is that why you're being nice to me?'

Maureen held Mo by the hand.

'No love. It's not the only reason. The night in the shower, I thought he was kickin' lumps out of you and ye were, well . . . at it.'

'"It," is that what they call it?' asked Mo.

And they got another fit of laughing. Maureen told Mo she wanted her to be the daughter she never had.

Mo didn't lift the death threat there and then but she did call out to Maureen's house later that night and took Dermo off death row.

Mo phoned me the next morning with all the news. Mo would find time to speak to me while her husband was up at the runs feeding his dogs, and kicking things.

Mo was kind of, but not completely, worried about wishing Dermo was dead. Back then, I couldn't see any logic at all in the Law of the Wish.

'How could you kill by wishing, Mo? There would be no one left, given all the hate that's in the world. Just check the net. It's full of people wishing death on other people.

Thousands of years into the future the archaeologists digging up Twitter will come to the conclusion the people who lived in the first decades of the twenty-first century were a truly horrible bunch of psychopaths and wish-killers. I lose faith in online humanity. It depresses the crap outta me. So if people are so bad how come more of us aren't wished to death?'

Mo seemed a little calmer. Or less rattled, might be the best way of putting it.

You'd never know with Mo.

She could go through hell on earth and somehow manage to get by. Mo never ever really had a sustained period of happiness, so when bad things happened to her, she saw the abnormal as normal. Men were shot in gangland feuds just down the road from the block of flats Mo and her mother lived in. All the while Mo studied, day and night, just to get out. Mayhem and murder and drugs and drink were part of everyday life. There were good times, but the bad times were never too far away, and the gestation period was an instant.

You made for home, head down, no eye contact. The bad boys and girls were on their rounds in their souped-up cars or taking up both sides of the pavement with hoodies up.

There were many more ordinary people who just got on with living their daily lives.

I was never there. No one ever did go, bar the people who lived in Mo's home place, and people who worked for the government.

Mo told me how it was.

The people there did the shopping, brought the kids to school, went to work and made every effort to play the hand they were dealt. On the news the area was described as working class, but hardly anyone living there had a job.

The good people lived in the war zone, not of their making. Sometimes the innocent got caught in the crossfire while the rest of us parked our fat arses on white horses high on the hill overlooking the battlefield. And the generals always say, 'It will all be over by Christmas.' But decades of neglect, poverty and relative poverty have gone in too deep. Their troubles are layered now, like an archaeological site.

It's as if there were two countries, divided by a border, defined by postal addresses. If you were born in 4 you were fine, and if the number that came out of the pot was 12, well then that was you well out of luck. This was the second partition of Ireland.

Employers would give you the time of day and then lash off a quick email to say how impressed they were with your interview. Thanks but no thanks. We'll keep you on file. Just in case something comes up. Under F for Fuck Off.

But we were fine. Dad described the way it was back in the seventies when the war was full on in the North of Ireland. The people in the deep south, where we lived, 'Might as well have been on Mars.'

Dad told me, 'Some story might have come on the news about twenty people being killed in a bomb but even though the north was only three hundred miles up the road, it might have been in Afghanistan, for all people were prepared to do about it.'

Now the distance in the city between the safe places and the dangerous places is no more than a bus stop or two, but Mo's home is still in another faraway country.

Mo was even more unemployable because she dropped out of college when she became pregnant. The chances of Mo getting a job were somewhere between none and slim. But I didn't tell her that when we talked about the future. She knew. Mo knew, but she didn't complain. Because it would do no good.

'I took back the bit about Dermo dying. It was probably an accident alright.'

Ah well, forgive and forget that's what we always say when someone is the cause of killing a baby. But I didn't say that. It was in my head now, she would never leave him.

Mo spoke about the Law of the Wish.

'I know the Mrs D thing was probably only a mad coincidence anyway. But she did wish my baby dead and I wished her dead. And now they are both dead.

'Maureen kept going on last night about Hitler's astrologer who forecast the death of Mussolini and even his own death at the hands of the SS and Hitler's death in a bunker. It was all in *The Law of the Wish*. Maureen had a premonition she would be killed by an Olsen unless there was what the wish book called "an intervening event".

In the book there's a bit where Hitler's astrologer wrote out on a letter to his next of kin that he was going to die at the hands of the Nazis and one morning they called to his house and took him away. And, well, killed him. Just like that.'

'Jeez you're losing it completely now.' I turned the speaker on my iPhone all the louder. I just loved listening to that voice.

It was girly hoarse, sang too much, smoky and very gentle. Sometimes her voice broke and went less croaky and a little high. But her tone was always soft and kind. The kind of voice you would like to wake up to in the morning, even if you were really tired.

Her accent was a strange mix of inner city and posh. She could move the accent in either direction when she concentrated, depending on who she was talking to. Mo kept a special voice for me. An even softer and more gentle voice with a slow and easy rhythm, all of its own.

'Hey, G. Guess what dude? I was at his jigsaw again.'

Mo had prized away part of the wheel of a Ferrari from the framed jigsaw glued together by Dermo. The masterpiece was hanging over the mantelpiece on permanent exhibition. Dermo was very proud of his work. Dermo thought he not only put the pieces together, but designed the car as well. Every now and then he would ask what happened to the missing jigsaw piece and Mo would say it must have fallen into the fire when the glue melted.

There were several gaps in the huge jigsaw and the red Ferrari was badly in need of spare parts. Schumacher, the German driver who was standing by the car, had lost his crotch and Dermo coloured it in with a marker.

'Maybe I am losing it but I just can't leave. Not for a while. But I will go and soon. I still have nowhere to call home. It's going to take time for me to get well. Maureen gave out yards to Dermo. She swore it was really an accident and that he just kicked out and happened to get me in the worst possible place.'

I didn't know how to react to that. He kicks a baby out of her and she as good as forgives him other than to remove a wheel from his Ferrari and emasculate a cardboard German racing driver.

I would never have given her any excuse to forgive me for something bad because I wouldn't do anything bad.

Dermo would always be nice to her after acts of ignorance and violence. This time he sent an expensive voucher for a makeover. There was no way he would have thought of that all by himself. It had to be Maureen.

Did she think Dermo would reform?

Maybe Mo was always and forever about to give him one more chance.

The answer was in the future, but how much time can you gamble on someone beyond redemption?

There was a dependency in her too, I think.

The broken home she came from was better than no home and maybe the Compound was the same. And I didn't exactly jump in with an offer of a bed in my apartment.

But who knows what's going on in anyone's head. The only way human behaviour makes sense is if you accept we are all mad in varying degrees, with the Dermos right up near the top of the scale.

Western Europeans are descended from four or five explorers out of the Rift Valley in Kenya who made their way across the world, via a few million years, to the Compound. So it says on the TV.

Everyone is everyone's cousin. We are interbred and mutants of ourselves. Well that's my theory and some are madder than others. In time and with training and practice it's some bit sortable out. For most.

How we help each other out defines us.

But I feel so small, scared and useless. I don't really know what to do, to make us safe. It was sort of like trying to keep out the tide with a plastic chip shop fork.

Maureen is now Mo's closest woman friend.

One night, not long before the baby died, Maureen made drinking chocolate with marshmallows. She patted Mo gently on the belly.

'How is my little my grandchild and it swimming away without a care in the world? You must play nice music. Elvis would be lovely. 'Love Me Tender'.'

Maureen put her head on Mo's tummy and hummed a few verses of a lullaby.

'They can hear music in the womb you know. And later, when they gets older, they remembers it.'

I wondered what sweet music Mo heard in the womb. Shouting and drunken fighting I would guess, for certain.

Dad used to take me down to the river when I was a small fella and one day he brought home an orange-coloured toyshop net attached to a slender bamboo pole. We travelled hand-in-hand from our house to the Owenalee, over a timber style, and through two green meadows dotted with little yellow flowers.

I netted darting salmon fry in the lukewarm pools under the weeping willows at the lazy bend.

My Mam washed out a jam jar.

'In case the little fish get diabetes,' said Dad.

Mam laughed. She used to laugh at all his jokes back then.

I took the fry carefully from the net. They wriggled about tickling my palm as I closed my fingers into a tunnel, in case the fry fell off and were lost in the long grass.

Carefully I placed the babies in the jar.

The salmon fry died after a few days. I blamed myself for taking them away from their river.

'Ah, little G,' explained Dad, 'some are meant to perish and more are made to go. Only a tiny few grow up to be big salmon anyway. They have so many fish and bird enemies and they live in a very dangerous place.'

I grassed from an internet cafe, so deep in the inner city, it was an independent republic. A place where the citizens were allowed to get on with whatever it was they were doing, provided they didn't bother anyone on the outside.

Cameras owned every street. The police could trace an email sent from a laptop or an iPhone. I wore a hat and dark glasses at night. Like a rock star.

I was the only white person in the cafe. Walk into a shop in some other part of town and there was always the chance you would meet someone from home, or work, or wherever. In Ireland, there was only one or two degrees of separation. Except in Ethnicland.

The email gave the police the exact location of the Olsen place and a detailed account of the death of the Papillon.

More than a week passed before the cops got around to calling to the Olsens but by then the dead donkey had galloped off. The runs had been cleaned up. Bones were

42

buried, or maybe Dermo made consommé for the flask he brought on lorry trips.

Dermo must have had the captured dogs killed in one last savage waste not, want not orgy.

He produced state dog licences and breeding papers from the Kennel Club. There was no proof. No one ever exhumed a donkey or a Papillon and so it was, the Olsens walked. The Olsens were always breaking some law. Some were small laws like driving without silencers and more were big laws. The family sold stuff from their vans. Dodgy smokes and fake DVDs. You'd never know what they'd be up to. Maybe Dermo smuggled in drugs but Maureen hated drugs, so maybe not.

There must have been a tip-off.

Most likely the police made a judgement call. Which was more important to the law? High-quality intelligence, or a few stray dogs waiting to be torn apart on death row?

The Olsens were giving the cops information in return for immunity. Mo was sure of it. She often overheard Dermo talking to a Sergeant Matt. Dermo used to tell Big Matt, as he called him, about the criminals he met on the road, the stuff they were up to, where they were going, and why.

I was petrified and wished I hadn't sent the email.

But if they did trace me, would I be forced to testify against the Olsens behind a screen, wearing a bulletproof vest, with a new nose, and a digitally altered had-a-stroke voice?

I was truly horrified over what happened to the little dog. But I wasn't going to testify against Dermo. Not for a dog. Maybe not even for a human.

The stress of it all fuelled the mad dreams and worries.

Would I finish up on a witness protection scheme, somewhere in the Deep South of the USA? In a place where there were no Irish, and catfish gumbo stunk the house. With fuck all to do all day only swat flies with rolled up newspapers and flick the zapper until I get epilepsy or go blind from jerking off at porn channels.

In the end I give myself away with the emigrant's corny longing for home by going up to an Irish pub in El Paso and singing 'The Fields of Athenry' and asking for Chef Sauce with my corned beef and cabbage and saying top of the morning or whatever crap it is mock Irish people say when they greet each other in Hollywood movies.

Thor Olsen, a long-lost Swedish American lumberjack cousin, spots me from the pictures circulated by the clan all over the world. He cuts my head clean off with his axe. And sticks it on a barbeque fork, as a warning to the others.

Although on the positive side there would hardly be too many lumberjacks south of El Paso. Unless he was a cactus lumberjack.

As ever and always I began to lose it under stress. I saw all this in my mind.

The wide awake dreams were back.

Ridiculous as the odds were, I just couldn't turn off the stupid images, especially in waking time. It's like watching your operation on a TV monitor. There's no end. At least with nightmares they stop when you wake up the next morning and you say thank God, it's only a dream.

Which makes me the living dead. But my dreams are all action. I'm a frenetic zombie.

My Mammy told me I was always talking about 'pictures on my pillow' when I was a kid. She and Dad assumed these were my happy kiddies' dreams about Disneyland and stuff.

Mam thought it was kinda cute, but they were terrifying head movies of people being killed. Maybe it was brought on by the murderous TV we watched from the age of four.

Mo didn't know it was me who tipped off the police.

Even though I trusted Mo, you would never know what she might say to Dermo in the heat of the moment, just to hurt him, and not in any way to get me into trouble. Married people say stuff to each other they wouldn't dream of saying to anyone else in a million years. Sometimes I could hear my parents arguing late at night.

I used to pull my head under the bedclothes, until I nearly smothered.

Then one night my Dad pulled back the duvet, gently, and found me with my eyes closed and my thumbs in my ears. I never heard my parents argue again. Love left but courtesy stayed. For the kids' sake.

Mo knew it was him. From the sounds made by the dogs. He was a day early. She tried to hide her cases, but there wasn't enough time. Dermo always drove right up to the door at speed, as if he was trying to catch her at something she shouldn't be doing.

The dogs recognised the revs of Dermo's engine.

The Alsatians barked a series of warnings when an ordinary car drove into the Compound, but for Dermo they sang in a high manic pitch.

Grey, the leader, started the yodel. His pals joined in. The Doberman pups down in the far-off amphitheatre, led by their diva mother, sang 'welcome home, Dermo' in a howling wolverines' chorus.

'You're home early.' She forced a smile.

Dermo was almost always cranky after a long drive. Some c— drove out in front of him and he nearly jack-knifed, or the pigs pulled him over to check mud flaps and tacographs.

Dermo's road rage kept going when he wasn't driving. One wrong sentence could trigger him.

She was hoping he wouldn't notice the labelled cardboard boxes full of books on the kitchen table or the half-filled open suitcase on the floor of the utility room. Mo was getting ready to leave Dermo. Her plan was to be well gone by the time he came home.

Dermo walked past her on the porch, through the kitchen, to the back of the house.

She hid a suitcase in the broom cupboard.

'Dermos Den' was painted on the door of his private room in a large-lettered red daub. The letters bled into the door and dripped down in long, thin lines.

Mo was often tempted to stencil in an apostrophe, but thought better of it. The door was padlocked. Dermo nailed on a steel frame for extra protection. Mo always wondered what was in there.

A deep freeze for sure.

Dermo brought frozen bags of minced meat from the

Den. I joked that Dermo put hitchhikers to death and butchered them for dog meat and kicks.

Mo knew Dermo kept his stash of cash in the Den. Once when Dermo was out-cold drunk, Mo went through his pockets and found nearly six grand in fifties and hundreds. Supposedly thick people can add, multiply and subtract with the brightest, provided you substitute x, y and z for dollars, pounds and euros. Dermo had plenty of money.

'Strip, bitch!' he shouted in a weird, high voice. Mo dived on the sofa for her mobile. Dermo got to it first. Mo was sent flying to the floor.

Dermo squashed the phone under his big boot. The one he killed their baby with. He undid his shiny belt buckle.

'Not now. It's my period.'

And she smiled at him again. Then with a shrug, she said casually, 'You know how it is with us women.'

He put his face in hers.

'I don't want to shag you,' he whispered softly, forcing his revolving tongue into her ear as he squeezed her slender wrists so tight she felt pins and needles on the tips of her fingers. He moved back a little and looked her up and down. Still holding her wrists in a tight grip, he whispered again.

'I wants to torture you.'

Dermo tied Mo's hands with the cowboy belt and dragged her roughly across the hard, tiled kitchen to the Den.

Mo tried to scream, but he got his hand over her mouth and muffled words into mumbles. There followed a vicious punch and Mo's left eye started to swell up almost immediately.

Dermo ordered Mo to stand up.

Mo was choking.

'Will you shut up if I let you breathe?'

She nodded. Mo stole a breath. She felt absolutely helpless and under his power. Mo kept on thinking her way through the ordeal, trying to figure out how she could escape unharmed.

'Swear on your dead baby you will shut your big fuck-faced mouth.'

Your dead baby. Your dead baby.

That ate her up. The 'your dead baby' bit. Your. Your. Your. Your. But she kept quiet. Mo was screaming inside but she nodded again, barely able to propel her head forward.

He took away his greasy black hand from her mouth. Mo drank in the air in big gulps. The breaths tasted of diesel and sweat.

Dermo opened the door of the Den.

The door was stiff and stuck. The timber had contracted from the damp and cold of the Den. It made the hoarse throat noise of a door opening in a haunted house movie. Dermo kicked the reinforced door with such force, he knocked flakes of caked black paint off the wall.

He took out a bag of minced meat from the freezer and ordered Mo to put it up to her eye.

'You'll tell the Ma you fell?'

She nodded again, afraid to speak, and not trusting her squashed voice box. For Mo it was just a case of getting to the next minute without getting hurt and taking it from there. It was all about survival until he wore himself out. She stood in the centre of the room with her head lowered and her hands joined. Mo prayed silently. A long prayer to Holy Mary the nuns taught her.

'You bruise easy,' he said in a calmer voice.

Dermo lit up a cigarette even though she never saw him smoking up to that. But it was only an intermission. He put the cigarette out by stubbing it slowly in Mo's arm. She screamed loudly and tried to free herself from the cowboy belt.

'Shut–the-fuck-up.'

Dermo hit Mo across the face with a leather motorbike glove as if he was offering her out for a duel.

He rummaged through the drawers of a bashed-in filing cabinet. Mo could see the nostrils of a shotgun sticking out of the half-open bottom drawer. Dermo took a cordless drill from the top drawer. She bought it for him for his birthday. Black and Decker. Mo thought it might help to domesticate him. The drill buzzed before Mo like as if he was inscribing the airspace in front of her with threats.

'Open wide. It won't hurt a bit. It's just like giving head.' He slapped his thigh and laughed hysterically at his own joke.

Dermo took an egg timer from the credit card pocket in his motorbike jacket. He push-kicked Mo over to a purple chaise longue that might have been the property of a Madame or a broke property developer.

'Admit it and I might go easy on you.'

'Admit what?'

He straddled her. Placed the egg timer on her heaving and contracting chest. Dermo picked up the egg timer with his mouth and pressed it into to her forehead, leaving a perfect red circle.

Then he showed her the sands in the top chamber.

'This is how long it will take me to rape you, bitch. That's all of my valuable time I can spare. When the beach is down in the bottom half, we'll flip her over, and then you'll get what's comin to you.

'Now for the nineteenth time, tell me it was you what ratted on your husband who has been very, very good to you, givin' you a good home and a new kitchen. And you as good as an orphan with nobody to look after you. Your husband what is a lovely man, what has a big heart, a heart as big as a turnip, dey all says.'

'I haven't a clue what you're on about.' And she didn't.

'I know you know. It was you what done the grassin' on us bout the fightin' dogs. But we weren't caught, cunt.'

Dermo stopped, as if he was thinking, and scratched his head with his left hand as his right hand pinned Mo by the neck to the chaise longue

'Howld, howld on now. Ah but I'm all wrong there. All wrong. Wait up. Whoa up. A cunt is a useful thing.

'The cops was tolt everythin' what happened. You sent it. You sent it. That fuckin' email. You betrayed your husband you swore to love, honour and obey up in the altar before the priest and before God hisself.' Dermo was crying as he spoke. He slapped her hard across the head.

'Bitch!' he shouted.' I used to love you. I fucking used to love you.'

Semi-concussed, she saw stars. Actual stars. Shooting around in all directions, like in the cartoons.

Mo didn't move. Lay as quiet as could be. She knew he was out of control now. He was still sobbing, silently. And feeling very sorry for Saint Dermo The Victim.

She braced herself for another slap or kick. Her head started to clear a little.

The last grains of sand shifted to the bottom chamber.

The epileptic drill rat-a-tat-tatted a drum solo on the thin-assed antique George the something chair. The crying stopped.

Dermo turned off the drill and asked quietly, 'If it wasn't you, then who was it?' He was blinking rapidly as if the single bulb hanging from the ceiling was hurting his eyes.

Dermo sat on the antique chair. It broke under his weight and he stayed on the floor with his head in his hands.

Mo was shaking but years of crisis management enabled her to put on the face again. Dermo was having one of his migraines. He twisted and turned from the pain. Dermo rubbed his knuckles into his eyes. He got up and sat down again on the floor. Experience and instinct told her now was the time to risk all.

'You are a dead man if I wish you dead. Even if you kill me, my curse will get you. Just ask your Mammy. I killed more than Mrs D. Did you know that? I can kill whenever I like. All I have to do is wish. Just a wish and you're dead. But I don't like killing people unless I really have to. Unless I really have no choice.'

The fury squirted out of him. It could be he believed Mo didn't know about the raid, which she didn't. Possibly he saw the headache as Phase 1 in his death by wishing. Maybe he was afraid of his mother. Or was some little bit of human still left in him? And did he still love her? It could be random, down to the route the roulette balls took round his head before they stuck on a saner pocket.

Dermo stood up, slowly.

'Get the fuck outta here. And don't never threaten me again. You're not worth doing time for, bitch.'

Mo released her hands by pulling open the belt with her mouth. She put on her top. It was one of Dermo's and had 'Route 66' embroidered across the front.

She walked out slowly. Route 66 was hanging just above her knees which were scratched and bleeding from carpet and tile burn.

Dermo squeaked, 'You know I was going to bring you to Route 66 on the honeymoon.'

She closed the already swollen eye and made her way slowly and silently towards the door. Mo counted every step, scared that if she ran, Dermo would sense her fear and might strike again. Mo's wrists were so bruised and sore, she could barely open the door. She glanced back at him.

He was lying on the chaise longue, his head busting from the pain.

Mo wasn't sure if she had won, or if this was a truce, or just a postponement of the inevitable.

Mo told me of her ordeal in the Den. In the

way you might tell a scary ghost story on the night of a power
failure by a flickering candle.

Butterflies with razor blades for wings flew round my
stomach as she spoke.

If she broke down and told him I was there when the
Papi was slaughtered, Dermo would have tracked me down.

We planned her escape and hiding. Maureen, unwittingly,
set us up for a meeting.

Maureen, who was hoping Mo would never leave, organised it with Dermo that Mo's college friend could call. Me
that is.

'They were only butties,' Maureen told Dermo, and I
was 'only a small, little country lad who might talk a bit of
sense into her. He's a friend only and he might be a small
bit gay.'

There could be no jealousy of someone as small as me.
Or as gay as me, even though I wasn't in any way gay. Not
that there's anything wrong with being gay, just for the
record.

Eventually he gave in.

Dermo was at home in his mother's house, where he was now living after a truce brokered by Maureen. He must have been watching out for me all day.

Grey ran up to the door of the car. He licked my shoes. I was afraid he would bite me.

Dermo was laughing.

'Don't worry, Runt, he won't ate you. There's not enough flesh on you. He must like polish. Why did you polish your tiny shoes anways? Sure they'll only get dirty again. Are you tryin' to ride the wife by any chance? Is that it? Dat why you're all dressed up? '

Dermo went down on his knees and smelled my toes. 'I'm on my way. That polish has me buzzin.'

He stood up. Sniffed me all over like a dog.

'Oh you smell like a chemist shop. Fucking hate pillow biters. You wanna dem lads? Ha? Ya?'

He caught my head in a vice grip, as in the TV wrestling.

'Smell that. That's a real man.' I was suffocating. The sweat was sickening. Luckily I was so nervous I didn't eat before the visit.

Dermo grabbed my hand and walked me to the door as if he was bringing a child to school. It was humiliating. He squeezed so tight the tips of my fingers turned white as a dead man's.

White as my dad's in the coffin.

I needed my Dad. What am I doing here, Dad? In the middle of all this shit. How did I ever get into this?

I prayed to my father.

'What's in the bag, Runt?' Dermo asked.

We were on the porch by then. He was still squeezing my hand. I didn't tell him stop. Mo came out.

'Let go,' ordered Mo.

Dermo squeezed even harder. I went on my knees with the pain. I have small hands. My mother wanted me to become a vet.

'Let him go. And call off the dogs. Now.'

Whatever it was she did to him in the Den was still working in some part. Or maybe he was trying to get back in with Mo and beating me up definitely wouldn't help.

Dermo went away somewhere in a big old Mercedes.

Mo showed me into the house.

She rubbed my sore hand gently. Already there was red bruising. The hot tea she made helped and the warm cup brought the colour back to my crushed fingers.

I brought Mo a laptop and an iPhone.

She cried and I was sort of glad there was no 'ah you shouldn't have' or 'I can't possibly'.

'Thank you so much, G. This is freedom.'

'It brought down governments.'

When Mo moved in, the Olsen house smelled of dried-out wet dogs and syphilitic cats.

Mo scrubbed and cleaned until her hands went raw and numb.

There were fresh flowers in every room and eventually Maureen persuaded Dermo not to bring the dogs into the house.

Mo never had any money of her own to do it up. But it was very clean and had Mo touches everywhere. There were bookshelves with books on them and nice matching prints of happy kids shovelling sand on a sunny beach.

Mo spread out the drawings she'd made of her dream kitchen.

'There will be an island in the middle and the paint will be warm like a kitchen should with a big table and eight chairs, so all the family could sit around and talk.'

'Eight? Wow!'

She laughed.

'Yeah, G, eight – six children plus two parents. I was always on my own. A latchkey kid. Like in the song 'Nobody's Child'.' I started to sing the first verse of the maudlin ballad. Dad used to sing it for laughs in the pub, just to get the oul wans bawling.

'No, G don't, it makes me too sad.'

Mo stapled pictures from magazines onto the kitchen design sheets. There were kids everywhere and rocking horses, baby chairs and toys scattered all over. Some of the mag pages were old and faded. One was dated ten years ago and I asked Mo if she thought six kids was enough.

Mo laughed. 'Stop, G, I'm serious. Six children would be just right and we could spread them out so there would always be a baby in the house and all the older kids could look after the younger ones and learn parenting skills.'

Dermo bought a stolen to-order flat-pack kitchen for a grand and a mate of his, who learned carpentry in prison, installed it for two hundred euro, while Mo looked on helplessly at the botch job. Maureen had the taste of a whorehouse decorator. The sofas were mock leopard skin, matched with orange curtains and wall prints of motorbikes and *The Last Supper* in cheap plastic frames.

'I want teak and granite,' she said. 'Something that will last forever. Like my marriage. The next one. Obviously.

'I'd love an Aga. I would keep that stove so clean and shiny and bake my own soda bread. And I would leave the windows open so the kids could run in from the garden when they got the smell of a freshly baked loaf and I would give them a slice and the butter would melt on it making it extra delicious. Oh yeah and G, the garden would have trees and a swing. But the kitchen is the centre of the home. There would be an old style country dresser with blue and white delf in every press and we'd keep a special set for Sundays and visitors. And a comfy sofa with room for everyone to snuggle up under a blankie on cold winter nights. And teddies everywhere. For hugging and comforting and not just looking at. And a man who will love me even when I'm doing stuff I shouldn't and forgive me after, without going on too much about it.'

I was going to say her dream home was close to mine, but I didn't. And that I was that man who could make her happy, but I didn't say that either.

Mo made a broccoli bake and garlic bread. After we had coffee and homemade apple crumble with whipped cream. I thought it was a really good dinner from a woman who never had a proper mother.

She told me the flat that I helped arrange for her was still there. Social services held it over but only for another week or so.

I had to get her out. Somewhere in the background was the thought that there was no escaping from him. But if it was dangerous to leave, it was even more dangerous to stay. The only long-term solution was to get Dermo locked up.

'Have you ever thought about going to a solicitor? Dermo will have to pay alimony. The cops will send him away for years after what he did to you.'

Mo turned away as she walked back into the kitchen with the dishes.

'I know, but I have stuff to do. And some day he will get out. If I did shake him down, he would just kill me or have me killed. He knows people who do hits for a few grand.'

I followed her in with the plates.

'What stuff have you to do?' I asked.

'There's Maureen. I like her. Love her.'

Maureen made the truce, but Dermo was only a door away. He promised never again to touch her but he hadn't kept his promises up to this.

'But you can't stay just because of her. Dermo will go back to his old ways soon. The fear of being killed will wear off, the longer he stays alive. You don't believe in that wishing by killing crap anyway? Do you, Mo?'

Dermo sent a new dishwasher by way of reparation. Mo filled the dishwasher as she spoke. She accepted the peace offering because the dishwasher was the only part of her life 'where everything has its own place.'

'The knives went into the knife section and the big plates slid into spaces like the ones they park bikes in at school. The cups and mugs were suspended on spikes. And at the end of it all, the cups and the knives and the plates were clean and ready to be put back in the drawer. So there.'

Dermo saw what had happened as just one of those little marital tiffs, like in his own home life as a kid, and he promised Mo a tumble drier as soon as one fell off the back of a lorry.

'Come on, Mo, surely you know the wish-killing is just nuts.'

'Not really. Well maybe just a bit. I don't know. It's the same as not believing in ghosts but being afraid to sleep in a haunted house. If you know what I mean?'

Then she showed me a torn-out newspaper piece. *The Law of the Wish* was at number 1.

We talked. Mo told of the night her mother came home drunk with a friend and the light bulb swayed in Mo's bedroom. The force of the sex sent the headboard of her mother's bed banging against the walls. I was honoured she told me such a personal thing. I could see Mo never had any grace in her life and she was trying to talk out the bad memories to make room for new ones. Happy ones. I never loved anyone as much ever. I wanted to make her dreams come true.

I told her about Dad's singing fish, which beat the shit out of *The Law of the Wish*.

His name was Big Mouth Billy Bass. The fish was real looking, well to a kid anyway. Billy twisted in time with the music and his mouth opened wide into a perfect O as he sang slow and hoarse.

You could sum up all the self-help books in the world with the song Billy sang – 'Don't Worry Be Happy'.

'It's as easy as that, isn't it, G?'

I told her before she asked. Or it could be she trusted me to tell her in my own time.

'It was me who tipped off the police about the dogs. I am so sorry, Mo. I should have known it would come back on you but I was just so upset about the cruelty. And you didn't tell him it was me, even though you must have suspected.'

Mo was almost flippant.

'I sort of guessed it was you.'

Mo walked me to the front door. It was dark by now. The moon was a cradle for a baby. Mo's hanging flower baskets swayed gently in small arcs like a kiddies swing. Chinese bells tinkled a tune composed by the soft wind.

There was a pause. Not for long, because I was edgy there, out of doors, or half out of doors.

Dermo could be hiding out behind one of the old cars the Olsens used for spare parts. The dogs could be crouching, hidden anywhere. Waiting to pounce.

She sort of looked at me in that special way they look at you.

'Hey, G. I'm nearly better. Everywhere. You know . . .'

Her eyes not looking to see my reaction. Shy almost.

Mo slipped out of her shoes, elegantly.

'Look, G, look, we're the same height. As good as.'

We were but I still had my shoes on.

I was shy. Didn't know what to do or say.

'Call to see me soon and don't be scared.'

There was an awkwardness for a few seconds.

She kissed me on the lips.

As I left and was walking towards the car, delighted with the kiss goodbye, but ever wary of the wolf's cousins, she called out:

'Hey, G, forgot to ask, what's *schadenfreude?*'

I kept on walking backwards or sideways on my toes, in a circus horse movement. All the while scanning.

'Some German expression to do with revenge. Something like that. I think.'

I could have checked straight away on my iPhone but

Alsatians can be sneaky, being related to wolves and all that.

'You can Google it now,' I advised, from the safety of the car, with the window down, but not all the way. Just open enough to hear and speak through, like the gap in the cashier's counter in the bank.

She waved goodbye. In the wing mirror I could see her standing there in the porch.

I drove out the cattle-gridded exit and past the new sign that read 'Bewear of Dermo'.

There was a quiz for retards on the car radio.

Yipee G, you win a weekend for two in your own house.

The old man would swear if he ever won a weekend for two on the mother's radio show, he would ask to change it to two weekends for one. Not that he would ever ring in. But he will not be calling up. Will he? Sometimes I forget my Dad is actually dead.

I wished I didn't think so much. Wished I was in an automaton's job, like putting toys in a cornflake packet.

Wished I could just have savoured the kiss without worrying about the consequences or the intent.

Wished I was answering easy questions on the radio phone-in, like spell CAT.

I sang a song aloud. About me.

> *It ain't easy*
> *It ain't easy*
> *Bein' Tommy G*
> *Wo wo wo*
> *It ain't easy*
> *It ain't easy*
> *Spellin' C-A-T*

That's it, the song that is, and you sing the same verse over and over again. For the sad verse you just sing it slowly.

The car was held up at the lights.

I Googled Schadenfreude.

It means taking pleasure out of other's misfortunes.

Mo was playing a very dangerous game. Dermo failed playdough in Junior Infants but his instinctive hunter's instinct would instruct him when it was time to strike out.

And as for poor Mo, well she was afraid to go and afraid to stay.

Mac Sorley Homes went bust without warning.

Owed millions. They were our biggest builder clients. But I held onto my job. Just. Mostly everyone in the construction business felt this was what was called an 'adjustment'. Whatever that meant.

Mac Sorley's collapse was the beginning of the worst recession in decades, but it wasn't a recession, even though the building industry was falling in on its own foundations. At the start the experts called the recession 'a soft landing'. As if the recession had the landing gear of a cat.

Whatever it was, I might soon have to look for work abroad.

The boss tendered for a job in Saudi, which never appealed to me due to the heat and lack of pubs. Then I got to thinking, and the upside was we would be safe there from the Olsens, who surely wouldn't try it on in a country where they chop off your hand for wanking. I wondered if we would be kept in a Compound guarded by dogs. There was no way I could live in a place with mad dogs and no pubs.

The owners of big mad dogs have a want in them.

As if they needed the dogs to scare people and not because they loved the dogs, like say a sheep farmer who loves his Border Collie and who might even go on the telly with him, on one of those sheep herding programmes, with whistling, and the owner and the collie on first name terms. No one ever heard of anyone going on the telly showing off a Doberman. Unless alone they hired him out as an extra in a prison break movie.

I had these terrible fears Dermo would set the dogs on me. On the news there was a story about a little boy who was ripped apart by savage dogs. I had seen what had happened to the Papi. It was a phobia now.

Dermo told Maureen I was a threat when he came back from the horse races, just a few days after my visit.

'If dem little jockeys can ride a thousand kilos of a horse travellin' at forty mile an hour, well then the Runt might be able to ride my missus lying on the flat on her back.' Maureen just laughed it off, but the story made me more scared of him than ever.

I think Maureen told Mo the jockey line, to let her know Dermo was jealous of me. And that he was very witty or humorous as well. Jealous meant he still fancied her and wanted the marriage to work. There was no way we could've figured that at the time. With some people, and Maureen was one, you have to examine their every move and every word as there's always a motive or a plan.

Safety pushed me for Saudi. Mo would be dressed up like an old nun. Except for me. Exclusivity. She was wearing see-through knickers and bra. You could hang wet crombie coats on her nipples. I was driving when the image appeared in my head but I could still see the road. The car swerved as I drove and the fantasy died.

The kiss put the stamp on it. It tasted of longing and love.

It was then I decided not to leave Ireland. Messed up and all as it is, I kinda like it.

We were touring Brittany in a hired out motor home, with Mam and Dad, on our summer holidays. It was about ten at night in this big town called Pont something with eight eyes in the bridge. All the lights were off in the houses and even the pubs were closed. Dad said there must have been a curfew.

Then he came out with, 'It's no wonder the French have the name of being such good lovers. They're in bed half the night.' He was a journey shortener with gags and quizzes and stories. The twins didn't get it. They were too young, but even Mam laughed at that one.

Dad explained he used to bring us on foreign holidays to show us how good Ireland was and that we should try to stay at home when we were big. Make a go of it. He used to say it would be great if we could live near each other when I grew up. I was delighted Dad wanted me to be near him always.

I'd miss calling to his grave if I left Ireland.

He died at fifty-three.

My mother was probably an accomplice, or guilty of murder in the second degree. Everyone is a killer. We all kill each other. Either in one go or incrementally. Mam killed Dad with her constant nagging. Our mother was very good to us and to everyone else but she didn't really like my Dad. I think they fell out of love through being bored with each other and getting annoyed by small things, like Dad putting his feet up on the coffee table and her smoking in the house. We didn't live in a Compound but Dad and Mam did.

At first I used to pray at his grave with a flurry of Hail Marys, said so quickly they blended into each other like a closing concertina.

He died when I was nineteen. Now I go to talk to him. Bring him all the news.

I look up at the hill behind his grave, as if he's sort of up there, wandering about in some form we have yet to figure and then I look at his new Compound and sometimes I think it's not really a compound at all, and Dad is free at last. Maybe I just imagine those messages from him are coming into my head. I suppose it is a kind of hereafter when the thoughts of those who die are with us. In that sense part of them is in us. My Dad lives on through me and his influence on me.

I visited Dad's grave the morning after the kiss. We got to talking, or maybe I was a ventriloquist talking for the two of us, but I do believe he is present when I tell him my story. One of his sayings was never judge a man until you walk a mile in his moccasins. I was scared of the Olsens. So. Then I thought I shouldn't be too hard on myself. Walk in my shoes and see if it's easy.

My mother didn't really like Mo. It went back to my twenty-first. The morning after the party, Mo was sitting cross-legged on the sofa in what my mother called 'the lounge'. My mother was like a bitch as someone got sick the night before in the sink of the en suite.

'Get your feet off that sofa. You wouldn't do that at home would you? Then again maybe you would.'

Mo wasn't even wearing shoes.

There were half-awake, half-asleep partygoers, my friends, scattered all over the floor and on the chairs. Mam had an audience and Mo was so embarrassed and isolated, she turned scarlet.

But that was my Mam. She just came out with horrible statements and then she forgot all about whatever wound she inflicted five minutes later, but the object of her rant didn't. Ah man, but when my Mam humiliated Mo, it was like a nail scraping glass.

Mam was on local radio, on this discussion about women's issues. I was never so embarrassed. Mam said an educational movie should be made for Irish men, because all the Irish women were buying dirty books, not so much for the porn content, but as sex manuals. The ladies on her show laughed hysterically and so a star was born. Mam was given her own show.

'The set,' she said in a different accent to the one she used at home, 'would be a giant vagina and we could get Sir David Attenborough to walk through it pointing out erogenous zones and G spots in that educated, excited but whispery voice he puts on when he spots a stripeless zebra or a new species of armadillo.' Her guests were in stitches. I switched stations.

It was three months before I came home from college with the shame of it. Dad ignored *The Woman's Hour*, other than to say it kept Mam from asking him to lift up his feet when she was hoovering, while he was watching the racing on TV. I felt really sorry for Dad. Would everyone think Dad was bad in bed? The sex talk still goes on in *The Woman's Hour*. Dad isn't alive to stick up for himself now that he's dead. If Dad was alive he could put anyone down with his gunslinger repartee.

And then it upset me even more that all the locals would be listening to what should have been private. But at least he was dead for most of the shows.

Mam never left Dad alone, constantly controlling and bossing him. He usually gave in and kept quiet, but every now and then it all became too much and the arguing started. Mo and I never argued and we told each other everything. If Mo was having a bad day I just backed off and gave her time to sort out whatever it was that was bothering her.

Dad used to dodge Mam at every opportunity. 'Your mother repeats more than the worst case at any gastroenterologist clinic.' Mam maintained Dad couldn't face reality.

Dad said he could but not all the time.

They only spoke when she corralled him into one space, which was usually at meal times. Dad would have won a prize at a quick-eating competition. He horsed back his food and was gone before Mam could get stuck in properly.

Mam never tortured me much, except maybe around the time Mo came down to stay, or in small ways like asking me if I knew the facts of life. Mo took my mother's dig very much to heart. I apologised with a take-no-notice-of-the-mother. Mo was self-conscious of being who she was back then, and coming from her part of the city.

My mother kept going on and on with 'like in any man's language' and 'I don't know the half of it' and 'in my day' and 'what's the world coming to'. That was Mam. Torn between being a modern mam talking about sex on the radio, and an old-fashioned one, who was liberal for everyone except her sons. Looking back on it now, I think she wanted another her for me. Which I'm sure is against some law or is at least seriously unhealthy. But that's what she wanted. My mother.

Mam meant well.

She worked hard at keeping the house going and when the twins left for Perth she gave them seven K, which was probably most of her ready cash.

Dad the philosopher had a theory. 'There's only one frontier left and that's the mind and it's the only place where you can escape to.'

Mo was trapped and now I was too. We could dream all we wanted but we could never dream away Dermo.

There was always Oz. Dermo might not bother to go to the trouble of following us there. He might just see it as an expulsion from the land of our birth, and that was a strict enough punishment in itself.

Overlooking the cemetery was a low hill, with the ditches knocked to make more grazing for cattle. There was one tree left in the middle of the mini-prairie. I always looked up there to mark time, to remember when last I was here by reference to the leaves on the tree.

That tree was a remembrance of my Dad. More so than the gravestone.

Mam wanted a dice-throw of white marble pebbles on Dad's resting place. Dad asked me to make sure only grass grew over his grave. It was the only time I got the better of her. I told Mam I liked to smell the grass when it was cut for the first time in the spring. I'm not sure what would've happened if I told her Dad wanted the grass, so I made up that line about the scent in the spring.

I stood there, talking away to him. Not aloud but in my head.

Dom Dooley came over to Dad's grave to say hello.

Dom was dad's pal from school. Dad used to call him Dom Pérignon because he had a very bubbly personality.

'Tough times, G but if the good times don't last forever, neither will the bad.'

I just nodded. Everyone knew everyone's business in our little home place. Dom knew my job was down to three days a week.

'Do you know what your oul fella said about six months before he died? We stopped right here to say a prayer at your grandparents' grave. "Pérignon, you go along without me, sure it's hardly worth my while going home."'

That was him alright. Dad laughed at death as well as life.

I left the grave with the implanted thought from my Dad that it wasn't my mother who would be going out with Mo. It was me, so Mam would just have to deal with it.

The oul fella looked at life as if it was bewildering and totally random, but very funny at the same time.

That did it for him but I had to figure it all out. Try to sort it in some way. He was an observer and that was easier. Dad was always positive. The fact that I had a special drawer for my socks meant that I would be okay and wouldn't lose things like the deeds of the house, which he did, much to my mother's annoyance.

My mother was strong and opinionated. Dealing with her would not be easy and I was wondering if the El Paso lumberjacks would lend me a chainsaw to cut the umbilical cord.

Maybe I'm not being fair to Mam and Dad. It wasn't that we were unhappy growing up. It was just that it wasn't perfect. But we had a chance, a very good chance of turning out alright.

Dermo got into the habit of tagging along with Maureen when she came to visit next door.

Mo was uncomfortable, but because of her relationship with Maureen, she just about tolerated him. Mo didn't speak to Dermo, who was unusually quiet and walked a few paces behind his mother.

Maureen passed the marriage problems off by calling it 'the silent treatment' and told Dermo 'you had it coming'. Like as if he was out with the boys and didn't come home until 4 AM. Torture in Olsenville was no more than being a bad boy.

Maureen was a peace-keeping force and so Mo wasn't afraid of Dermo, as long as his mother had him by the hand. Mo knew too, if she left Dermo and the Compound, Maureen wouldn't be around as a human shield. He would find her and take his revenge. Maureen's little boy had a big ego. If word got out Dermo was thrown out by Mo, then the other criminals might sense weakness and try to get him back, for the horrible things he must have done to everyone and anyone. If Dermo couldn't have her, well then no one else could either. And what would he do to the someone else? Could it be Mo was thinking of me and my safety? That the *schadenfreude* excuse was just that.

Mo figured Dermo would eventually meet someone else and then, under the rules of the game, she would be free to go. Mo would be the one who was rejected. It was a case of hanging in there until he did find the someone else.

Dermo had sworn off the drink, according to Maureen, and he was going to the gym every day.

Then one day, Dermo arrived in to his former home on his own. Out of the blue, as usual. Maureen was in the city getting her hose-pipe varicose veins diverted into a culvert.

'I'm here for our jigsaw, Missus. I bought another one the same kind on the ferry and I'm takin' the pieces what's missin' and putting em inta our wan.'

Dermo must have thought he had served his time, and that now he was entitled to move back in with Mo.

She asked him to leave but he ignored her. Mo couldn't help herself. It just came out of her mouth before she could stop.

'And it's not our fucking jigsaw, it's yours. Your jigsaw. Now get the fuck out before I call your Ma.'

Dermo hummed in a bluebottle monotone as he walked non-stop from one side of the living room to the other.

Dermo's eyes were red, bloodshot. She always knew how he was mentally by looking at his eyes. Mo didn't make full eye contact. It was a surreptitious look. No more than a glance but she knew from the way his eyes darted about like a swallow, Dermo was out of his mental mind.

Mo got to thinking it wasn't drink or coke this time. It might have been steroids. Bought in the gym. His arms were huge now, like thighs. 'Roid rage was common enough among the Dermos who needed to be bigger and stronger than everyone else.

When Dermo peed in the kitchen sink, Mo knew it was the end of *schadenfreude* in our time. That was how his dogs marked territory, by peeing everywhere. Maybe Dermo had spent so much time with the Dobermans, he had turned into one himself. This was him reclaiming what was his.

There was a tiny window in the bathroom. It worked on hinges and did not fully extend. Dermo could not have suspected Mo might escape that way. There wasn't enough room to squeeze out, but Mo had already loosened the screws on the catch. Weeks before, Mo hid a screwdriver in a plastic bag in the cistern. There was a fifty euro note in the bag, a spare mobile phone and a Stanley knife. She removed the screws quickly.

Mo climbed out the bathroom window. Head first. For a few seconds, she was hanging upside down, with her insteps curled round the window frame, like a circus acrobat swinging off a trapeze. Somehow Mo managed to swivel her legs round and she wedged her left foot against the cement casing surrounding the window.

Bit by bit, Mo crabbed down. She jumped off the windowsill from a standing position. Grey was watching her every move.

The old mongrel walked with her until they reached the gateway out of the Compound. Mo ran the roads until a taxi she called picked her up about a kilometre from the Compound, just off the intersection with the motorway. Mo spent the night in a hostel for women, who were victims of violence in their own homes.

Dermo kicked in the bathroom door, smashed the cistern top and promptly left for Le Havre. It would be a week before he came back. Or so Maureen reasoned.

Maureen, along with Dermo's brother Mikey, collected Mo in a café near the hostel, the very next day. She didn't call me.

Mikey warned her.

'He's gettin' worse. He's goin' to explode. Can you go? D'you know, for a while like you know, until the polis comes? I'd call them if I was you. You can get him barred out of the house. Official like. Mam dunnit to Dad wance and it quietened him.'

Mikey looked over to his Mam for support.

'For a while. He was quiet for a while, Mikey,' added Maureen.

Then Maureen took over.

'We have a good friend. He's Sergeant Matt and he will come here to fix things. Dermo respects Sergeant Matt. Doesn't he, Mikey?'

Mikey nodded.

Maureen put her arms on Mo's shoulders and looked at her in the eyes as she spoke.

'The Law of the Wish could kill Dermo and maybe you too. There's nottin in the book that says no one can't kill you, love.'

Maureen convinced Mo that Dermo was definitely away in France and he wasn't coming back. She spent the night in the Compound.

Mo asked, over the phone, if I would help her to escape.

I hesitated for a few seconds. To figure out what I was going to do. Well maybe it was a bit longer than that. It was my move but I didn't move. If we were to live together, I would have had to have time to figure it all out. Pick the apartment. Pay the deposit. Sign up for the electricity. Alarms. CCTV. Random stuff. Check if we could afford Sky TV and make sure the bins were collected weekly. And I hadn't even asked her. I was just assuming. Crisis management wasn't my strong point.

Mo was a quick person. She waited for me to respond and must have figured the delay was a no, or a can't-make-up-his-mind. She was instinctive, and I tossed ideas around in the mixing bowl in my head forever.

Mo made the decision for me.

'No, wait a couple of days. I'm in terrible pain. Just can't move. Complications, from losing the baby and climbing out the window and the shock.' Or so she said. But so often Mo told me she was fine physically.

'Okay,' I said. Too easily.

'Anyway,' she said, before I could put my thoughts on a list, 'the police are coming in the morning to take a statement.'

Mo was out of ammo now. Her short-lived scaring of the beast was over and forever. She had to leave. Staying was impossible. Leaving gave her a chance. For a while anyway. A head start.

'But where will I go?' She sounded like a kid lost in the woods. Scared of the Big Bad Wolf.

Mo was just a little older than a little girl.

'Don't worry. We will find somewhere safe. Another hostel or something. I might be able to organise someplace safe. Soon enough. Or I'm sure the police have safe houses.'

Safe. Yeah, through a witness protection scheme, organised by me, who wasn't cut out for conflict. And the victims of family violence aren't exactly likely to be given new lives and a permanent pension in Tahiti.

Fuck but Tahiti wasn't even safe. All those places with palm trees and golden beaches eventually get overrun by tsunamis, dictators, homicidal jellyfish and sex tourists.

And 'soon enough' was something like the plumber would say and you both knew he had no notion of calling for ages, if at all, and only then if the chimney was the only part of the house that wasn't covered in water.

All the while, there was the constant and real dread of Dermo. Fear was really keeping me away from her.

What if the Olsens threw a petrol bomb in the window of our house?

Or stuck a firelighter at the end of a knitting needle through the letter box that didn't have a stiff moustache for protection?

It was on the net. About a bomb attached to a toy chopper that was piloted in through the chimney pot by a mobster who must have been an expert in cybernetics and he blew the whole fucking gaff to smithereens and the people in it too.

The fact the police were coming gave me some comfort. Surely Dermo would be charged with manslaughter of the baby, the savage attacks on Mo and maybe even cruelty to the dogs. If Mo's evidence alone would be enough to convict him on that one.

That would be the end of the danger for a good few years, or so I persuaded myself at the time. If some day in

years to come he did get out, the odds were prison would
have emasculated him and his rage and the madness would
be either decreased or gone. That was how I saw it, or
wanted to see it back then.

The police called to the Compound, as promised.

The main man went by the name of Sergeant Matt and
the omission of his surname gave him that kind of trusted
friend of the family handle like Father Tim, who was
probably grooming the kids, or Doctor Harry, who was
pumping antidepressants into the mother because he
couldn't be arsed listening to her and there was a queue in
the waiting room. I didn't trust any of them, any of the
same old guys who ran the show into the ground. Any of
the guys who used words like 'decremental' when the country was in freefall and jobs were getting cut by the day.
They were all such a bunch of fucking conmen and liars.

Good old Sergeant Matt made a big speech about respect-
ing women. He happened to be the very same Matt
who played Dermo, his pet stool pigeon. By an amazing
coincidence. My arse.

'First we will get you a Protection Order, pet,'
announced the Sergeant, who was probably surprised Mo
didn't puppy lick his fingers in thanks.

Mo wasn't a bit impressed.

'My name is Mo.'

Sergeant Matt was that fond of himself, he wasn't even
listening. He slid his wide, cow's tongue around his
swimming ring lips and into the far-off corners of his
mouth, to get a taste of his own wonderfulness.

'Then in a few weeks,' he continued, 'we can get a Barring Order. Which means, per se, Dermo cannot, under no circumstances whatsoever, enter into the house or the cartilage thereof. If he so much as looks at you, looks at you,' and he peered out at her over the tops of his glasses, 'we can bang him up in a cell. Forthwith. So to speak.'

There was shine off Big Matt. He was red. The light reflected off his florid face. He wasn't as big as the name suggested and Mo suspected the 'Big' bit in Big Matt was put in by himself.

He spoke in a formal voice, as if he was taking an oath.

'Sorry, Maureen, my dear, we are aware of your admirable maternal instincts but the law is the law and Big Matt tells it straight, straight as a pencil. Big Matt will keep the peace. So help me God. That's what we are there for. Garda Síochána means custodians of the peace and Big Matt, who was once a rookie, believe it or not, many years ago, and when he was in that humble state and still a young man, he swore an oath. A sacred oath, in the presence of the Commissioner of an Garda Síochána and the Minister for Justice to uphold that sacred duty, without fear or favour, from that day forward, all the days of his life, until death do him part. Big Matt would not forsake his oath from that day on. Thus, most definitely, he would not. Big Matt would take a bullet for those under his protection. Oh most certainly he would.'

Big Matt looked at Maureen with eyes as round and bulging as pool balls attached to tooth picks as he thanked her for the little drop of whiskey she handed him at the end of his speech.

Maureen swore her Dermo was still out of the country.

'It wasn't just pretend,' she said. He left France for the Isle of Man motorbike races.

The first thing that came into Mo's head was the high number of deaths among the bike tourists who attended the TT races. Stupid gits who got their kicks from scaring the shit out of blue tits and farmers on country roads and ended up killing themselves and whoever happened to be unlucky enough to get in their way.

'You were right to go to the Guards,' Big Matt opined assuredly, as he sipped the little drop which went up to the rim of the tall Slim Jim.

'No woman deserves that, whatever the provocation.'

'Provocation?' asked Mo. She stood up now. Mo was livid.

'It wasn't me who was the violent one. Hello.'

The officer straightened himself. Back went his shoulders and out went his big belly.

'Hello to you too,' greeted Matt and he continued. 'In the course of my preliminary enquiries, Dermo steadfastly maintains you did threaten him. With death my dear. With death. The ultimate sanction. It is his word against yours. If we follow through with criminal charges, then a file will, in the normal course of events, have to be sent, after due diligence, and proper forensic dissection, to the Director of Public Prosecutions himself, or to one of his lawyers properly invested with his authority. It won't be up to us by jingo and I often wish it was. It all comes down to what's in the file. The file never lies unless there's lies in it and Big Matt don't tell no lies nor write them either.'

'How can I be brought up?' asked Mo, who was overwhelmed by the fact she couldn't even trust the police.

'For threatening his life, my dear girl. A serious offence indeedy my deary and punishable by a long term of incarceration in the 'otel with no carpets.'

Maureen had been nibbling away at her red-tipped, bitten-down finger nails, as she always did when she was nervous. Playing for both sides was placing a terrible strain on her nerves

'Listen to Sergeant Matt. You will be safe now,' comforted Maureen.

'Mikey is very fond of you,' she continued, 'and sure he's well able for Dermo. If Dermo ever touches you, he'll never darken my door again. I told him as much. On my life. Mikey isn't that right? Mikey.'

Mikey looked at his mammy and nodded earnestly, several times.

Mo could barely talk with the shock of being account-able for wishing death on a wife beater and a child killer.

'I didn't threaten to kill him. I just wished he was dead. And that was after he killed my little baby. He's the one who should be up for murder.'

Big Matt took off his Garda hat and rubbed his shaven head with both hands in a downward motion as if he was parting what was once growing there. Then he moved his left hand down to his left ear, part of which had been removed either by a bite or a passing bullet.

Having massaged his ugly bits, the great man of the law went back to conducting police business.

'That's another day's work, my dear and I can assure you no stone will be left unturned if indeed there are stones to be turned,' pontificated Sergeant Matt, loudly mounting every word to stand on its own.

'I will send one of my cars for you at about ten, exactly. You have nothing to fear, my dear. You are now under Sergeant Matt's protection. Safe as houses you are,' according to Matt, very much unaware houses were halving in price by the day and falling down from pyrite, and bad boom-time workmanship.

'Now my dear the first hearing will only take five minutes. It is a formality. And all in private. I had a word. In the right ears. Dermo does not even have to be present before his worship.'

The word present must have reminded Maureen.

'For your wife,' as she handed the sergeant a large bottle of vintage French brandy.

'Ah there, there, there. Now stop. There's no need of that, Maureen. I couldn't possibly.' Big Matt had his pneumatic eyes fixed on the gold label on the bottle and his hands extended to accept the gift.

The notes in his notebook read well. Job done. Source protected. Wife shut up. Missus gets a bottle of brandy round as a potbellied buddha. Matt was in line to be Superintendent Matt and Dermo was his point of personal distinction. His very own exclusive source.

The ould fella always told me you'll never beat the Sergeant Matts of Ireland.

'It's like this, my old friend. After their big win at the Battle of the Little Big Run, old Sitting Bull told the celebrating braves to take it handy. Keep the head like. Not to be jumping about sporting the scalps on their chests like some young one who won thirty-four medals at the Irish dancing.

'You might lick a couple of hundred troops, advised

wise old Sitting Bull, and use Custer's blond hair to stuff a cushion, or line a hot water bottle, but there will be more to take their place and then more again if you beat them until eventually they will get you. They will never run out, but we will. There will always be someone to take their place but not ours.'

Mo got her Protection Order. The lady judge was very nice to Mo and pronounced she had only to call the police and Dermo would be arrested.

Maureen forced Matt to take a voucher for his wife's birthday.

'Ah sure weren't ye great to remember.' This was Mrs Matt's third birthday this year alone.

Maureen said, 'If you counted up all Mrs Matt's birthdays she would be 224 years of age.'

That night, I was back home and Mo was back in the Compound.

She was going to leave soon and maybe go to the hostel for a while. I definitely would call to collect her at the hostel and get her to a place where she would be well away from Dermo, who moved from the Isle of Man to Russia, to do some deal over there like maybe assassinate the President and the Prime Minster or train in dogs for the reopening of the gulags.

'Cool,' and that was it between us for a few more days.

I couldn't afford my flat in the city. I did have €13,707 in the bank, but the city was no place to be without regular money. Mo was only twenty minutes away from my place, but so were the Olsens. If I moved back home, where the living was easier and cheaper, Mo would be three hours up the motorway. But so too would the Olsens.

There has to be a difference between judgement and conscience. Judgement comes into play when you're looking at a job and are trying to figure out the price of stuff, like building materials. Your first opinion changes so much. You reckon a job might cost say a hundred K, and then when you get into the pros and cons the building project might come to another twenty K, over and above your original estimate. You make a judgement call. It's facts and figures, blacks and whites, mostly. You do the maths and measure the dimensions. Analyse and decide. Keep up the margins.

So in judgement your third or fourth opinion is always best. Not so in conscience. In conscience your first call is always right.

I knew from the very beginning it was up to me to get Mo out of the Compound but I didn't push it. If I really loved her, that is. I should have stood by Mo but Dermo wasn't going to be charged with anything. Maureen was clever. She pre-empted any move by Mo to go to the decent police by getting the Olsens' private cop to take care of the situation.

I broke the news to Mo over the phone.

'Mo I moved back home to save money.'

'When I get fixed up, I can sort you for the laptop and all the stuff. Get a loan from the credit union. It might take a little time.'

'Forget that. It's only money.'

She was crying. Or at least I think she was.

'I can still call up to see you every now and then.'

'Thanks.'

'You will be okay. Now you have the Court Order.'

'I might try to get work somewhere. I would do anything and then I will be able get you some money towards the cash you gave me for the tooth and the laptop and the iPhone.'

'Didn't I tell you to forget all that stuff?'

Mo's voice was a little angry now.

'I can't take it. It's too much. We're not talking about a box of chocolates here, G, you know. Just because I'm from the poorest part of town doesn't mean I haven't any pride or that I don't pay back my debts.'

It was only after the call ended that I realised why she was going on so much about the money. Could it be she saw us as being together and when I told her I was moving away, the tooth and the technology ceased to be community property?

I fixed up Skype for the mother, who was useless at anything tech or electrical.

Except for the time when Mam had six women review six makes of vibrators on *The Woman's Hour.*

Cringe. The shame of it. I wanted a Mam who was stupid and did stupid things like knit socks and iron jocks. And then again I didn't. Mam was brave and fiercely independent. I needed her to back me up when life became too tough.

The twins were starring on my tablet. Mam was so delighted to see their smiling faces. It was a great comfort to her. Seeing the boys made me wish they were here with us. They badly needed a talking to and I'd love a pillow fight.

I wondered if they were putting up a show or were they really buzzing. The two of them were pushing left and right, trying to get more of their heads on screen. Telling me and Mam about the good life in Australia.

'Two weeks in the bush, G and back to Perth for five days in the bush. Wo.'

Mam didn't get that one.

Or if she did, she said nothing.

The twins were almost fully qualified welders. Then they would be on huge money. Like maybe as much as two grand Australian a week. When I heard what welders were being paid, I knew for sure Oz was next to be fucked.

Home was fine. Nice dinners and my own bed. Mam and me, and she had no one else to spoil. No hassle, no driving for hours to travel short journeys as in the city. But there was nobody my age around. It wasn't just the lack of work that sent us away; there was no one to hang with. All gone to Oz or England. Or to the States. The village was an old folks' home.

The Bourke brothers shuffled up the street to the post office to collect their social welfare on their flat feet. One was called Five To One because his toes turned inward and to the right, at an angle corresponding to 12.55 on the clock. The other brother was known as Ten Past Two, as his toes were turned out to ten past two.

Later they will get drunk and the Gardaí will tell them to go home and stop acting the bollix.

That used to be the highlight of the week in law and order. Because they were on the dole, the local sergeant called it state-sponsored terrorism. Then out of nowhere the young lads started to do dope. You can get any drug you want within five minutes. It's even quicker than the city because the traffic isn't that bad.

But I was safer here. The bad lads knew me. I was at school with the mad boys, used to play football on the same teams. They wouldn't bother me unless I was really unlucky. Like as if I was standing outside the chipper in town and was picked on because they were doped up, or got caught in the crossfire when they started to kick the shit out of someone, or maybe hit on a friend of yours who owed them for grass or shagged some girl they were into. You had to be unlucky though and if you kept your mouth shut, that should keep you out of harm's way.

I continued with the calls to Mo, but not every day. More like every week. Our calls were shorter now. Mo was always just about to head off somewhere or Maureen was just after coming into the house or she needed to keep credit for a call to the hospital. I sent texts. You get out of intimacy by texting. Even if it's just by forwarding a joke, the illusion of keeping in touch is maintained. We didn't laugh as much anymore. I was away from it all now. Safe and fairly happy. We were drifting apart but there was no big bust-up. It was like the economy was supposed to be. A soft landing.

Two months passed by as quickly as scrolling through an online airline calendar.

Maureen moved Mo into her holiday home on the beach.

Mo was fairly sure Dermo was persuaded to go for psychiatric help for his drug, drink and steroid addiction. Maureen, in answer to Mo's questions about Dermo's whereabouts, said he was still in Russia but Mo guessed he was away in Ireland, for treatment, probably at Sergeant Matt's insistence, as part of the deal for keeping him out of jail. For sure Sergeant Matt would never become a Super if his protégé murdered Mo.

But then one day Maureen asked Mo to get her stuff together, quickly. He was due home from wherever and they went for a drive to the seaside.

Dermo knew about the house but he thought it was rented out. Mo seemed happy enough there and she invited me to call up to see her. By now I had made a clean break and I was determined to stay away for safety's sake. My safety.

Life was boring but I needed boring. For a while.

Back home the pace of life was as fast or as slow as you

wanted it to be. There was no getting swept along and it was nice for the mother to have some company, now the twins were gone.

I picked up a few small jobs. Designed a hay shed for one man and applied for planning permission for a neighbour but there was no work and I knew it was only a matter of time before I too would have to leave this place I loved so much.

Uncle Andy was a builder in London. With the Olympics coming up, there was a few months of work going and he was always on the look-out for a good engineer, which really meant he was always on the look-out for a crook to cook the books and fry his punters. London had ten times more people than Ireland. There was always building of some sort going on in London.

You could finish up doing time over my Uncle Andy. My mother's brother was so into bribery, he used to drop the singers on the Tube a tenner to sing Irish songs. Uncle Andy had Rasta buskers in King's Cross singing 'Danny Boy' and 'Mother Macree'. Uncle Andy was always trying to proselytise the English.

Uncle Andy was fond of me. I was the *iachtair* in the litter according to Uncle A.

Meaning I was the weakest of all the family. But it wasn't my fault that my mother smoked twenty a day while I was wallowing unawares in her womb.

I was smoking a pack a day, at minus six months. I suppose I'm lucky to be as tall as I am.

Mo probably went for Dermo as a boyfriend, as opposed to me, because he was bigger. We were in this old castle and the door lintels were so low. The guide told

Mam and I the people of Ireland were smaller in the twelfth century. It was the only time I ever had to bend down going in a door. Man but I'd have been called Longshanks back in 1199 AD. It all proves conclusively the big survive. Dermo was tall and strong and handsome with all that Swedish blondness or whatever inbred fucking Viking fjord it was his ancestors came from.

There's nowhere, anywhere, safe is there?

America was out. Green cards were like gold dust and jobs were scarce there too. Since 9/11 the undocumented Irish lived in constant fear of being expelled from the States.

Bahrain were given the 2020 Olympics. There was work there too. Uncle Andy told us the Irish builders would be fucked if the Olympics were ever cancelled.

Saudi might be best. If it comes to that. From Mo's point of view it couldn't be any worse than the Compound. It mightn't be that nice for her though having to cover up. Her legs were straight and perfect. And it would be safe for Mo. But then we would have to come home some time and the Big Bad Wolf would be waiting for us.

It's all in *The Law of The Wish*. When you think about someone, that person comes into your life.

I hesitated. But then I answered her call.

'G, he's out in the back lawn. I can see him now. He's walking towards the house. Grey is barking like mad. I'm getting a knife, G.'

'Never mind the knife. Call the cops. Cut me off and do it now.' What can I do? Fly in like Superman and save her?

Mo turned the phone camera on Dermo who was a haze, a far-off shot in a mockumentary.

'He's outside the back window. His head is up against

the glass trying to look in. The eyes are popping out of his sockets.'

Dermo fixed a speaking collar on Grey. It was like one of those talking Barbie dolls.

'How are you today?' asked Grey in a deep, slow tenor voice.

The talking collar spooked Grey, who kept revolving his head until it almost snapped as he tried to get at the collar.

'I am hungry. Let's eat. Yum yum bones,' said the collar.

Dermo screamed a hysterical laugh.

Dermo jumped on Grey and caught him around the belly to stop him turning round and round in the same way a cowboy catches a calf for branding.

Mo was hysterical. 'There's no one living round here. It's a freakin' ghost estate. This whole place is deserted.'

I took a deep breath, sure that if I said the wrong thing, it would cost Mo her life.

'Call the cops quick. Now. 999. Or is it 911 or is that America? It's 999. Quick, Mo. Quick.'

Mo must have been moving about. The home movie was all a blur on the little screen.

Mo was before me again.

'I pulled across the bolts Mikey put in. What if he breaks in? Kicks the door down? Record this. Please I want a record. Please, G.'

The camera pointed to the floor and the walls and the ceiling and then out the window at the dog.

Grey asked for a drink of *wawder* in an American accent.

'Gimee the address,' I shouted, 'and I'll phone the cops!'

Dermo had gone out of sight, and Mo was in front of me, yet again, like a reporter from the war on the nine o'-clock news, but without a flak jacket or a helmet. She was flushed and petrified. Mo was panting between words and sentences.

'Mo will you phone the cops? Please. Do it now. Gimee the address and I'll do it.'

Dermo tried his key but Mikey had changed the locks.

'He's leaving. I think he's leaving.'

I could see Dermo's big frame, hunched, walking away from the house. Cut to Grey staying put on the porch.

Dermo turned round suddenly.

'He's still looking this way. He's laughing. He's turning away again. He's turning back again. The loony is playing games with me. He's looking at me looking at him through the front window.'

Dermo moved closer and closer to the camera.

'Phone the fucking cops! Phone the fucking cops!' I shouted.

Dermo was smiling madly into the iPhone. A close-up. He was out of it. His mad head filled up the screen. He was on stuff. Must have been. Had to be. I prayed in my own head. More Holy Marys for Mo.

Dermo lifted Grey from behind, under his forelegs, up to the level of Mo's face and on cue the dog collar sang, *'How much is that doggy in the window?'*

Dermo dropped Grey roughly and walked away again as if he was in a hurry. For a moment Mo thought the police had come into the estate. Grey didn't follow. He was hurt from the fall and Mo could hear the dog howl in pain above the twang of the collar wishing her 'have a nice day'.

Dermo ran back towards the house, at full speed, and pulled the speaking collar from around Grey's neck. The collar spoke rapidly as if Grey was possessed by demons with sentences running into each other.

I am hungry. Have a nice day. How much is that doggy in the window? Yum yum bones.'

Grey limped away from Dermo on three legs.

Dermo head-butted the window but it didn't break.

He smeared his bloody forehead round and round the glass. Mo had a lump hammer she found on the ghost estate. With both hands she swung it at the window. The momentum of the downswing smashed the reinforced double-glazed glass. Dermo's head recoiled as if he had been whiplashed.

She kept the camera on him.

It was impossible to see properly through the broken, bloody glass. Mo's shaking right hand made her movie seem like it was shot during an earthquake.

'I want to record it all,' she said calmly. 'You are my witness. If he kills me, you know who did it.'

Dermo threw the blood from his interlocked cupped fingers onto the window. The screen went redder as the streams of blood streaked down the cracked and broken frame like a delta. Mo pushed her thin hand through the letterbox and filmed Dermo running from the house. As he ran he screamed, 'I'll kill you, bitch! I'll kill you!' Mo told me Dermo drove off at a mad speed.

The series of dangerous bends is about eight kilometres from the holiday home on a winding, twisty coastal road. Dermo must have taken the wrong route to the hospital or maybe he was trying to get to a criminal who was also some sort of paramedic. Mother Aloys was on her way to see her brother in the Home. The Mother drove 'in my time,' as she was fond of saying.

Mother Aloys was eighty-seven. She shouldn't have been driving but the Convent insurance was still a big commission for her broker and the Mother bullied him into adding her name on to the policy. It seems Mother A was named after a martyr who was fed her own hands by some tribe of pagan cannibals but refused to renounce the one true faith even as they forced the finger food in her mouth.

With a name like that to live up to, Mother A wasn't going to give way.

Dermo and Mother A met for the first and only time in the dead centre of the Kilnaboy Road. It was calculated from the length of the skid marks burned into the tarmac that Dermo must have been doing around 160km per hour.

Dermo's car was heavier than the old nun's tin can. It was an old souped-up Merc. A tank.

Dermo braked. Too late. Physics killed Mother Aloys. Her almost severed head hung down on her right forearm. Dermo was knocked unconscious by the impact and there was blood everywhere. Old and new.

The nurse was on her way to work. One look was enough to confirm the Mother was dead.

The nurse climbed the stone wall and into the field where Dermo's Merc ended up. She tied her scarf into a tourniquet and managed to limit the blood flow. If the nurse hadn't been delayed by a stop-off to buy her favourite American-style Buffalo wings, which were really chicken wings, Dermo would have bled to death. If only.

By the time the ambulance came, Dermo was nearly all

out of blood, but he was still alive. Just about.

Grey was licking Dermo's blood off the cement path by the broken window. Mo took what was left of the now silent collar from around his torn neck.

Sergeant Matt interrupted the clean-up with a call. 'My dear,' he said, his voice quivering with emotion, 'I have the most calamitous news. Dermo, your husband, is in mortal danger. He is as near to RIP as he will ever be. It is not looking good, my dear. We may lose the poor fellow. Would that Big Matt was a surgeon, but he chose another career in which to better the lot of his fellow man. Mo, Mo can you hear me? Hello. Hello.'

'I can hear you.'

'He has lost a lot of blood. I have offered my own plasma selflessly to your husband, Mam, but alas it is the wrong type. Do you want to come over to the hospital? I can send one of my cars and believe me, my Garda will drive like hell. My men would die for me. Maureen and Mikey are on their way, as we speak, from the Compound. Only say but the word and I shall have you by his side. By his side I say.'

Mo, the possible husband killer, chaperoned by the police to the victim's deathbed. Good one, that.

'No, no. I'll stay here, if you don't mind.'

Sergeant Matt hadn't told her Dermo had been in a car accident. So Mo kept scrubbing. The sweat pumped out through her but the work kept her from going crazy.

There's no privacy anymore. Every call, every text can be traced.

Here I was on the phone to a woman who could be in the frame for the murder of her husband. I watched a home movie of the last minutes of a man about to die.

It was also going through my cowardly head, I would be seen as 'the other man'.

It would be death by tabloid or death by Olsen.

The red-tops would use words like bonk and love rat. Phone records would be checked and the calls I made to dodgy phone lines would be out there.

It wasn't as if I ever made dodgy phone calls to sex lines. Well just once and then I stopped. Who was I talking to on the other side?

It could be some perv playing with himself and putting on a girl's voice or an oul one of ninety pretending she was a young one. Seriously gross, and then you're paying about a tenner a minute.

They could check every email I ever sent to Mo, including some that were very critical of Dermo.

There was one, I think, where jokingly I suggested Mo should shoot him and she would be fined a tenner by the judge and warned to behave herself in future or she would be in serious trouble.

'Mo,' I gushed, 'I'm a . . . I'm a . . .'

I couldn't think of the word.

'I'm a . . . as in a handbag.'

Mo was calm now. She was making tea.

'It's an accessory, G. Stop panicking, will ya. It was self-defence. I had a court order. Jesus, G will you stop. Call you soon.'

Mo went back to cleaning the blood-stained cement with a scrubbing brush and washing powder. Grey stayed with her. She called a handyman who used to do odd jobs around the Compound. He couldn't come straight away. But he would be there first thing tomorrow, which in handyman talk could be at five in the evening, or a week later, or never.

The handyman came to fix the window later that day. By then Mo had sprayed the area in front of the house with a power hose.

'I heard about Dermo. I'm sorry. I came the minute I heard.'

'Ah well, we're separated. Can you fix the window?'

The handyman asked Mo if there was an accident what with the blood smears.

'Grey tried to get a fox,' Mo told him. Grey was hardly going to contradict her now that his batteries had run out. The bruised dog sat by Mo's side, quietly licking his wounds.

The handyman made himself at home. He sat at the kitchen table and sipped a coffee before he spoke.

'I know you and Dermo were split up but it must be still be a bleedin' shock. Jesus that oul bitch was completely on the wrong side. She's stone dead. Dermo had no chance. Ploughed right into her.'

The handyman took out a box of Olsen own-brand Marlboro cigarettes from a pouch on the front of his utility belt and lit up. He got up to measure the frame. The window was boarded up.

'Dem modern foxes would nearly sit down at the table and eat your dinner. I'll be back tomorrow with the glass. That nun. I knew her well. She had a brother with Alzheimer's up in the Home. I done a few jobs there.

'She was half-deaf and had thick glasses like the bottom of a jam jar. The oul nun used to drive with her head up agin the windscreen same as a suction Jesus.

'Lookit, I'm not knockin' no one, but that Mother Aloys was an accident waitin' to happen.'

Mo felt herself go weak. She had to sit on the windowsill.

Mo curled up her toes so much she felt a cramp go up her leg. The piece of glass she squeezed cut her hand.

The handy man stubbed his cigarette.

'You didn't mind me smoking, Mam?' after he took a long drag.

The handy man put the decommissioned cigarette over his ear. I suppose he could hardly stick it under his ear.

'It's a recession,' and shrugged an *ah sure you know yourself and we're all in the same boat.*

' MotherAloys?' asked Mo. 'From who – sorry where?'

It had to be her Mother Aloys. The handyman confirmed her thoughts.

'She was your one what was the head nun over in St Mary's boarding school for rich girls up in Clandeboyce. I think it was Aloys. Yeah it was Aloys. Sounds like she was called after hubcaps or somethin'. Do you know what I mean?'

It was the hand-me-downs that killed the Mother.

Mo was a student for three years at Clandeboyce, a very expensive and exclusive boarding school. The nuns took in a few kids from 'the wider locality' as day pupils, to maintain the illusion they were carrying out God's work. Mother Aloys was fond of saying, 'The well-off are God's children too.' Which was true, in a way, as God was looking after them much better than the poor kids. Even if he did have a change of heart after Ireland went bust.

Mo passed the entrance test with flying colours and her mother went on the piss for three straight days to celebrate the scholarship. An I wasn't such a bad mother now was I sort of a piss-up. She drank the back-to-school allowance, which was given by the government to parents to help out with buying school uniforms and books. There was no money left for Mo's uniform. Mother Aloys arranged for hand-me-downs.

Twelve-year-old Mo knew straightaway it was a second-hand uniform. Her mother told her no one would know it wasn't new. Mother Aloys sent a thank you note to the mammy who gave her the uniform, mentioning Mo was the recipient, and all about her family circumstances. The kid who had worn it the previous year read the note when she was rummaging through Mammy's bag for cigarette money.

Mo was teased from her first day in the school and left at the end of third year for a Community School in the city. It was pre the big take-off of social networking sites like Facebook and Twitter. So the bullying was all stored in head memory only. Mo either forgot or blanked out the details of most of it, but the girl who found out her secret never left her alone. She was cruel. Took off Mo's accent and sent her notes like 'Why do you always smell? Does your mammy wash your sanitary pads?' Then there was the taunting, 'Your mammy is your sister. Your mammy is your sister.'

The girl gave Mo a nickname – Eeny Miney.

Eeney Miney Mo
Catch a skanger by the Toe

If she screeches let her go
Eeney meeny miney Mo

Mo used to cry until the pillow was that wet she had to turn it over. Mo's revenge was to finish top of the class. Mo could not remember if she wanted the nun to die. Most kids wish death on some teacher at some time or another.

The handyman gabbed on and on but Mo took no notice. Mo was now seriously beginning to believe she had some kind of power.

Everyone in Ireland knows someone who knows someone but this coincidence of two on the death list getting their comeuppance, at the same time, in the same place, was still a long shot statistically. Like billions to one. Killing two birds with the one stone never seemed so apt.

If you added in Mrs D that made three. That's if Dermo was going to die and Sergeant Matt seemed to think he would, which was no bad thing.

If killing two people amounted to double murder then three would definitely upgrade Mo to a serial killer.

Mo Googled the FBI definition of 'serial killer' and all while the handy man was telling her Mother A had given him a fifty-cents tip, which he said was insulting and the Vatican should be sold off to help the poor, which no doubt included recession-hit handymen. Even there in the midst of an impending death he was setting Mo up for a big tip. She gave the handyman a tenner, just to get rid of him.

The FBI definition came up on her iPhone screen.

Serial Murder: The unlawful killing of two or more victims by the same offender(s), in separate events.

She was in. Up there with John Wayne Gacy and the Boston Strangler and Jack the Ripper.

Mostly the bullying in Clandeboyce took the form of copying Mo's accent. It could be Mother A knew this was going on and tried to fix the problem.

Or so Mo figured now, ten years later.

At the time she was really upset and miserable and Mother A must have picked up on that.

Mother A was an elocution teacher. Mo was soon speaking like a posh girl but it took some time. Mo never forgot the perseverance of Mother A. Her grammar was perfect after the three years but the inner-city accent never left her.

Mother A had her ways. 'Now girls, the organs of articulation are the tongue, the teeth, the lips, the soft palate and the lower jaw.'

Mo was brilliant at impersonating people.

'I nearly bit my tongue off trying to do the th's. I wasn't sure if I was being taught how to speak properly or give head.'

The nun drove Mo nuts but not nuts enough to have her killed by wishing, as was the case with Mrs D, unless it was a temporary wish, an off the cuff sort of adolescent wish that was never rightly cancelled. The old nun meant well and she gave Mo spending money for school trips, without ever telling her mother.

Mo was worried there could have been a disaster on a bigger scale. A bus sliding off an icy bend on the way to St Moritz for a Clandeboyce tenth reunion might kill fifty. She cancelled the wish immediately.

I told her not to worry too much. Most of the Clandeboyce girls' husbands would have lost millions in the financial crash and so the tenth would be held in a one-star motel with chicken leftovers recycled into an à la king for a main course, with soft stuck-together rice on paper plates with plastic knives and forks.

I was trying to cheer her up. It didn't work.

'He's going to die. I killed him. I killed another human being.'

Dora Seerly, who wrote *The Law of the Wish*, wrote that when death came she hadn't the slightest notion of disappearing into the bellies of worms. It was her intention to last forever in some shape or form. Through what Dora called 'The Doctrine of the Transmutation of the Spirit'. Because she wished it, her spirit would live on forever.

Dermo would never leave Mo alone either, even in death. The thought she had killed him even in self-defence might haunt her forever. Mo wasn't cruel in any way. She just wanted some love and a little peace. I tried to persuade her this was all just a random series of mad coincidences.

All three of Mo's alleged victims were doubly connected in life and death.

Mother A was in a pull-out fridge in the left wing of St Hilda's of the Holy Sepulchre.

Dermo was in the Intensive Care Unit, final home to the recently departed and little missed Mrs D.

The doctors were of the considered opinion that the next twenty-four hours would be crucial. Dermo had only a very slim chance of survival.

The car windscreen smashed but did not break into large pizza-slice pieces of glass capable of inflicting serious scars like those Dermo had suffered when he was wounded. It was more like multiple abrasions, as if he was riddled with an acne machine gun.

The Gardaí took the car away, as they do, to check out the brakes and that sort of thing. But would they compare the car damage and the medical reports? Mo waited and waited but it seemed the police were sure Dermo's injuries were caused by the car accident. She was in the clear, if Dermo died, and stayed unconscious until he died.

The doctors stitched up the throat wound. Dermo would be badly scarred, but if he was to die it would have been from the bang to the head. Dermo wasn't wearing a safety belt. Well he wouldn't, would he? Wouldn't have had the time to put it on while he was bleeding to death. He probably never wore one anyway, because it was a rule. But which bang to the head did him in? Was his trauma caused by Mo's hammer, his own head-butting of the window or the collision with Mother A?

Maureen and Mikey were on a bedside vigil.

Soon Olsens began to arrive from all over Ireland.

There was an injured jockey in the bed next to Dermo. He was in a bad way after a fall from a horse at a Point-to-Point.

Maureen came into the waiting room with the latest update on her son.

'At least he's not getting any worser,' was the prognosis.

The jockey's brother told his news within a few seconds of Maureen's communiqué.

The grieving brother lowered his head as he spoke. Tears welled in his eyes.

'The doctor says he's just about jumpin' the last.'

Dermo's brother Mikey had been chatting to the jockey's partner and she told him they had a two-year-old at home being minded by her mother.

'A horse?' asked Mikey.

'No a baby,' replied the jockey's partner tearfully.

That was Mikey. It was like the time Mo and Maureen were planning a trip to Tuscany and Mikey asked 'Have they elephants there?'

The Olsens were very nice to the jockey's family.

The jockey's brother and his partner were back in the waiting room within ten minutes.

They had bad news for the rest of the family. The jockey's mother broke down. His dad tried to comfort her but soon he too was sobbing.

The Olsens cried to a man and a woman.

Maureen embraced the jockey's mother. Mikey whispered to his uncles and numerous first cousins. They left the room. Mikey was back in minutes later. He called over the jockey's partner.

'Sorry for your troubles, Mam. The Olsens wants to show our sympathy. This is from us.'

Mikey handed her a large envelope with 'Blood Samples for Lab' printed on the front. Inside were the contents of the Olsens' collection. Nearly three grand. The Olsens had emptied their pockets.

The jockey's partner who was only nineteen said she couldn't take the money but Mikey wasn't for moving. 'It's for the small babby. He has no daddy now.'

Maureen told Mo there was one son who turned out good and Mikey's 'nature' helped ease half the regrets she had for staying with her husband.

The doctors were of the opinion the life support machine should be switched off. There was little point in keeping Dermo alive, the specialist advised, as there was no prospect of recovery.

There was no mention of a lump hammer trauma. It never came up at all. Everyone assumed Dermo was injured in the car accident. The fact Mother A's head was cut off implied that Dermo's injuries were consistent with a violent smash.

The blood tests showed Dermo had taken several

heaped teaspoons of coke, which explained a lot.

Maureen spoke to the hospital chaplain and he convinced her all this wishing to death was no more than chance and superstition. 'Dermo took cocaine and nobody forced him to. He was in rehab but he left of his own accord. It was his choice and his alone,' said the Chaplain. 'It had nothing to do with wishing anyone to death. It wasn't even the will of God but more a case of the will of Dermo.'

Numerous visits to the hospital church and the lighting of hundreds of candles brought Maureen back to her own religion and away from the teachings of Dora Seerly. Nuns consoled Maureen as she sat by the bed and they prayed with her. Maureen took out her Rosary beads and said Novena after Novena for Dermo.

Maureen practised a kind of voodoo-bling Catholicism.

Her house was full of holy water bottles from sacred fonts, saint's wells and blessed taps. There was a huge picture of someone who was supposed to be Jesus. He looked very sad.

Scattered here and there around her home, and outdoors too, were five mounted silver shrines to the Blessed Virgin. Holy Mary was dressed in real blue and white silk robes, embraced with golden rosary beads. The robes were covered in see-through plastic sheeting.

There were various mini-shrines to minor saints whose holy wells could cure blindness and arthritis. A black saint in the form of a doll was hanging off a hook on the ceiling. St Bridget was impaled by a nail to the rim of the shelf over the stove, just underneath a tea canister with two cute pusheens on the front and above a framed, signed photo of Dora Seerly.

The fridge was the coolest shrine of all. Stuck to the door were dozens of magnets of A-list saints, cathedrals, discredited Popes, several St Patricks and the thin-legged donkey from the flight to Egypt.

Our Lord's Sea of Galilee boat was berthed in a huge stagnant pond at the back of Maureen's house. The boat was one-fifteenth of the size of a real fishing vessel. The statue of Jesus was stilling the tempest and the seasick apostles were cowering. Maureen explained that Dermo bought it off a crooked orthodox churchman in Bosnia and brought it home with a consignment of dodgy cigarettes.

Mo moved back into the Compound two days after the accident. She didn't want the police calling to the holiday home in case the damage to the window was spotted and the blood analysed. Mo greatly missed Maureen. There was no danger from Dermo. Even he couldn't cheat death and because of the positive coke test, the killing of Mother A was now upgraded from a road traffic accident to a murder or manslaughter case. There was twenty-four-hour police guard on the Intensive Care Unit.

Maureen needed Dermo's good suit. To lay him out in. 'Wait there and I'll get it for you.'

Mo had Dermo's number-ones out of the wardrobe within seconds. The once shiny suit had lost its lustre and smelt of damp. There was a black Guinness stain on the back of the jacket, which didn't really matter as surely Dermo would be face up in the coffin.

I worked for a while in the Man's Emporium in Ballymore. The owner, Redser Doyle, specialised in bargain one-piece suit-shrouds. The black suit and the white shirt were back-less. The snap-on tie was clipped like a terrier's tail to just below the top button of the suit. The going away outfit didn't even have shirtsleeves. The cuffs were sown to the inside of the suit and there were no flies.

'Dead men don't pee,' was how Redser put it.

By the way, we buried Dad in his best suit from Italy. Goes without saying, that.

Maureen wasn't overly emotional. Eight days of crying drained her dry. She had come to the realisation Dermo was going to die and was ready.

Mo handed her the suit.

It was the same suit Dermo had worn at their wedding and the time he was up in court for spitting at a Garda.

'I must get this dry-cleaned, love. There's a two-hour place near the hospital.'

Mo began to cry.

'Where did it all go wrong?' she sobbed and Maureen embraced her tenderly.

'Go on, love let it all out.'

Maureen mammied Mo and Mo felt much better.

'Put on the kettle, Maureen. There's a cake in the fridge. Fudge. Got it for you.'

Maureen got to her feet slowly and made for the kitchen. They ate the cake, every slice, and drank numerous cups of tea with lots of sugar.

Maureen told Mo of how Dermo's Dad used to hang him off high roofs by the legs when they were stealing lead, just for laughs. One day he threw a hammer in the direction of Dermo and Mikey almost causing Dermo to lose his balance and fall off the roof. It was a wonder Mikey was as good as he was, she said, after all he had been through.

'And Dermo. Poor Dermo stood no chance. He could

be very nice. Only boy I ever seen or heard of what would make his own bed and he always put his plate in the sink after he finished his dinner. He had his good points.'

Maureen asked for Dermo's razor, the electric one.

'He got thirty-seven stitches and we haven't made up our mind if we'll open or close the coffin at the wake. His face is like a pin cushion and there's a terrible scar across his neck, like his throat was cut.

'I have Father O on standby and Masseys will get a horse and carriage to bring him on his last journey.'

I was brought to Lady Louth's tomb up in County Louth by this girl, Lottie, which rhymes with Totty, on a date. I swear. A freakin date.

Lottie was a bit off the wall but she was a Mo looka-like.

The crypt had been broken into by grave robbers and whoever patched it up didn't do such a good job. Lottie showed me Lady Louth through a gap in the front of the tomb where the masonry had fallen apart, just above the giant door slab of granite, with a rusted handle on the front.

Lady L was laid out in a ragged, faded yellow-white shroud. It might have been she was buried in her wedding dress. It had a back to it as you might expect. The Ladyship had been dead for fifty years but her hair was long and flowing and was only ever so slightly grey, even if her face was very thin.

Lady Louth's tomb got me thinking of my poor old Dad who shaved twice a day and now had no one to shave him.

He would have hated that. I take after him. Dapper, if I do say so myself. Dad was the first man around our place to buy a shaver for ear and nose hair.

The bikers would provide a guard of honour for Dermo and that was what 'he would have wanted'. She was afraid they might spook the horses but the undertaker assured Maureen, 'An earthquake wouldn't upset my horses. And I have earplugs as well, just in case.'

'Funny thing, Mo, but he said to me, they are human ear plugs even though you would think horses had bigger ear holes because they have bigger ears.'

That stopped Mo from crying. She laughed at the story. Maureen held her hand as she told it.

'We'll bury him with my father and mother, if that's alright with you, pet.' As if Mo was only dying to be buried with her husband.

'He was my son, Mo. Nothing can change that. I should have gone, but I had it in my stupid head his father would calm down and anyway he could be very nice to the boys other times. Most of the times.

'He would go off the drink for six months and everything would be fine. Then, mostly for no reason, or for some reason he only med up as an excuse and that some wan upsetted him, he would go back on it. I think he forgot, so he did, why he went off the drink or thought it was just a wan off when he got doped up and beat Dermo cross the legs with a bike chain. There was no stopping him when he was on the dope.

'Dermo and Mikey and me used to be shivering in bed

waiting for him to come home. There was no point in locking the door because he would chop it down with a hatchet if he thought we were getting the better of him. I'm not makin' no excuses. I'm only tellin'.'

Mo patted Maureen on her hands.

'That's okay, Maureen. I understand. Don't worry, whatever it is you say will not upset me. You are entitled to love your son, just as I loved my little baby who died in me.'

'If I coulda kept Dermo as a small boy, it would have been grand. He was such a lovely little boy, with his blondey head an' all. But there was always something about him. He was always fightin' at school and he could smile away at you wan minute and rear up the next.'

Mo had enough.

'Who are you tellin'? Sorry Maureen I wasn't being smart or anything.'

Maureen nodded slowly several times.

'I know that, pet. And oh and don't forget the electric shaver.'

Mo found the shaver under the bed, unopened in the box. She read the Christmas card without thinking.

'Too my darling husband Dermo. Happy Xmas from ure wife Moe. XXX.'

The writing was in Maureen's block letters. Mo was livid but then she calmed down and figured Maureen bought the card and the shaver to appease Dermo. For Mo's own safety? She was going to bring it up but changed her mind. Maureen had enough on her plate as it was and anyway Dermo would be dead soon, or so it seemed.

Mo ironed a shirt for Dermo. My mother, the feminist icon, broadcast on her radio show, 'No matter how big a bastard the husband is, the wife will always iron his shirt even when she knows he's only getting dressed up to go out to score with some other woman.' Or in this case a date with the undertaker.

Dermo was now in a coma for eight days.

I began to think he was staying alive out of pure badness. That somewhere in the darkness of his dead mind there was a tiny atomic particle of evil powered by a satanic energy.

The doctors gave up on the tenth day. The machine would be switched off at noon on Tuesday. Just in time for the doctors to go to lunch.

Dermo was clinically dead when a machine malfunctioned but he soon came back to life after the engineers changed a fuse or kicked the engine or whatever it is they do when life support gizmos go bad. It was touch and go according to Maureen.

Mikey played Dermo and Mo's wedding DVD in the Intensive Care Unit on Monday night. The background music was 'Every Step You Take/ Every move you make/ I'll be watching you,' sang by Sting, which if you think about is a stalkers' anthem.

Mo was interviewed by the luder who was doing the horror show DVD on the morning of the wedding as she was getting into the car to go to the church. Mo couldn't remember the script. She thought it might have been something like 'the happiest day of my life' as she sucked in to try to make her baby bump look smaller.

(Mo wasn't exactly replaying that DVD night after night.)

Then Mikey put on the highlights of the Isle of Man trip.

No one can tell whether it was the psychos on their bikes or the love words of his bride on the way to the altar that revived the dead man, but Dermo bucked up considerably.

It wasn't as dramatic as Jesus or Lazarus leaving the tomb but the doctors noted a definite improvement in his vital signs and he spoke, or tried to. His date with death was put back and the doctors put another coin in the meter.

Dermo came back from the dead. On the third day after he rose, Dermo was talking to the family about dog-fighting.

He was a new man. Born again. Vowed to change his ways. A priest heard his confession.

'This could be the answer to all my prayers. I never seen him so relaxed. He sat up in the bed and swore to God, he'd never do no more dope or drink again.'

Maureen was back as a believer in the Law of the Wish. She was certain and sure if the wedding video saved Dermo, then the marriage could be saved too. The book's 'semi-main premise' is: 'There is a reason for reasons. Connections connect.' Which was most profound of Dora.

Dermo also swore his second chance was a sign from God. He took Holy Communion every morning and swore 'swear to God' before every sentence, so as to emphasise he was telling the truth. 'Swear to God I'll never bate no one never again.' 'Swear to God I seen God when I died.' 'Swear to God he said "Dermo you're sound out. Sound out."' 'Swear to God I dunno what med me take dem drugs.' 'Swear to God I'm a prayin' for dat holy nun every day.'

Maureen was delighted.

'I wasn't listenin' to his confession, but I overheard him sayin' "Bless me father for I have sinned."

"Tell me your sins my son."

"Swear to God faaader but I done it all."'

Yes he did and the old priest forgave him immediately, on the spot. Dermo was given a penance of fifty Hail Marys but he couldn't remember the words or keep count, so his mother did the penance for him.

Marriage counselling was mentioned. A second honeymoon in a sunny place. The buying of a car for Mo. Dermo knew a man who could do deal on a cheap, trendy Mini Cooper. I'll bet he did. If Dermo was eating deep-fried hitchhikers and promised to stop, Maureen would have hallelujah'ed, 'Great news, our Dermo's gone vegetarian. He's after eating a big feed of quorn and fricafuckacee of sweet potato.'

My head is wrecked from the Dermo Lazarus story and his ascent into virtue. I had to spell check if there was an e after potato. Wouldn't that just be my luck? Dermo turns out to be a really nice fella after the bang in the head reconfigures his personality. I could see it all in my brain's screen.

Mo and St Dermo live happily ever after with heart-shaped flower beds and six kids and a swing. His loving wife washes his blond locks in the shower with jojoba and elderberry shampoo infused with camomile extracts. He sings in an Abba tribute band, being a Viking and all that. Then they all go to mass and sit up in the front pews, which would from then on be known as the Olsen Seat. Dermo gets up from the Olsen Seat at the consecration – the part of the Mass where the priest blesses the body and blood of Jesus Christ into the little slip of communion wafer. He takes the gold chalice from the priest, lifts it up as if he won a match and gives out communion to the congregation. Dermo who came back from the dead is a Eucharistic Minister and it's Easter Sunday.

Maureen kept up the prayers as a fallback position, but she was convinced her constant wishing as advised in the wish book – Chapter 13: Wishes Really Do Come Through (*sic*) – was working. Maureen told Mo the flow of positivity from mother to child, along some kind of cosmic umbilical highway, resulted in Dermo's resurrection and conversion. She wrote to Dora, who didn't write back. But Dora's theory explained all. It was in the book. The book was the word. Blessed is the book.

'The umbilical cord may be physically severed between mother and child at birth but the unseen energy remains and is a ready-made conduit for wishes.'

The Law of the Wish describes 'the phenomenon' as being similar to 'the phantom neuropathic pains an amputee feels in the toes he doesn't have'. The theory is, according to Dora, if pain can travel down invisible ducting, so too can mothering.

Maureen said Dermo would have to spend another month, 'at the very least', in the hospital but then he would be 'as good as new if wishes come true and they do'.

Dermo was, 'sittin' up an' aten a bit.'

Mo wasn't impressed. She knew only too well how quickly her husband could change from dormant to eruption.

Then, one wet morning, Dermo refused communion because the police and the nurses wouldn't let a newborn Doberman puppy into the ward. Dermo explained, 'That

pup's grandfather and father was personal friends of mine.'
Dermo told the priest he should have been wearing gloves
for hygiene during communion time. Told the nurse who
gave him the news about the pup she had small tits. Went
on hunger strike for a dinnertime. Pissed in his bed to mark
territory. And drank aftershave for kicks.

Dermo called Mo from a phone his mother smuggled
into the hospital in her knickers.

'Why didn't you come in to see me?'

Mo knew she should hang up but Mo being Mo couldn't
help but reply.

'I don't like it when people beat me up.'

'That's over. I was on dem drugs.'

'I'm glad you're off them but the Barring Order still
goes on.'

His voice turned squeaky as it always did when he was
off his head.

'Your barrin' order is a bit of fuckin' paper. Try stoppin'
me with paper. You only kill flies with paper and I'n not
no fucking fly. I need to get into the house. Now. 'Fore my
fucking head explodes.'

She could hear him inhale. The temper and badness
had him out of breath. Mo didn't reply. She was about to
cut him off. Dermo revived while Mo was figuring out her
next move. The rant continued.

'They wouldn't let me see my dogs what is fallin' away
to nottin without me. I need to get in the Den. I'm gettin'
what's mine, barrin' orders be bollixed. It's my house. You
only came in with the clothes on your fat arse.'

Mo wasn't afraid.

'If you come near the house, I can have you picked up

by the cops if you so much as look at me.'

Dermo laughed hysterically.

'Oh yeah an' are they after openin' a cop shop on the Compound specially for you like the president with twenty-four-hour guards with guns? It's gonna take dem twenty minutes to get to the house, bombin' it, and breakin' lights. By then I'll be in and out and you will know what's it's like to fuck with me. I'll do the time. I swear to God and I swear on my poor faader up in Saint Sepulchre's. I'll do the time with a smile on my face.'

Mo pressed record on her iPhone.

'Don't expect me to visit,' she said, deliberately egging him on.

'The solicitor told me I'm goin' down over drivin' doped up and killin' that psycho nun. If I kick the shite outa you, they'll just put it alongside the other sentence and the two will run at the same time as wan anudder. I'll get bail. I will. It's the law, I'm comin' home the minute I'm able, whether you like it or not. Sergeant Matt promised me he'll speak up for me and I might be out in a couple of years.

'And your wishin' me dead don't work no more. Cos I was dead but I came from the dead back like Jesus and whatshisfuckinface in the tomb. 'Cept I'm a fucking vampire now and I'll suck every drop of blood outta you until you have no more periods.'

She pressed red, deleted his number from her phone and blocked all calls from him.

Mo told Maureen of Dermo's short-lived conversion.

'He's had a bad bang on the head. There's bound to be setbacks.' But Maureen was clearly, deadly shocked and said hardly anything for a little while.

'Did you say something to upset him?' asked Maureen, umbillically.

'It doesn't matter whether I did or not. I just told him he couldn't come into his house. You can't threaten people and I'm not puttin' up with it anymore. No one does Maureen. I should never have given him a second chance after he killed my baby. '

Mo played the recording.

For a while there was a silence between them. Maureen left for her own house without a word but she returned after an hour or so with a hot water bottle and a blanket. She swaddled Mo.

'Do you know what I was just thinkin', love as I was talkin' and don't kill me for sayin' this, Mo.'

'I won't kill you for sayin' anything.' They laughed.

The tension between them broke. The women were left to pick up the pieces. Mo and Maureen knew they were in a world not of their making and so they had to make the most of that world. Mo knew too Maureen could never turn against Dermo, simply because she was his mother. Mo had a mother for the first time ever and Maureen made Mo into the daughter she wished she had, as some sort of a counterweight to all the men.

Maureen held Mo's hands as she spoke. To emphasise the seriousness and the truth of what it was she was going to say.

'I was only just thinkin' if the poor little babby got born. Well . . . well a little babby takes two to make and even if you split up, there's never ever really gettin' away from the Dada. You and the Dada will still be halves in a babby. Do you know what I mean, Mo?'

Mo nodded.

'And he would never let you keep it. He would just break you up in the head. Dermo wouldn't ever be able to bear the thought of someone else bein' the babby's Dada.

'And if the babby was a boy he'd get him on his side so that your son would go off with his Dadda when he was fourteen or fifteen and have some other woman for his mammy and I don't hold no truck with that but that's the what's what. Sure as I'm sittin' here. Dermo would bring him up so he'd always be in trouble and he'd never get to college like you even if he had your brains.'

'But,' said Mo, 'surely you can help. Please Maureen. You know he's crazy, but he is your son. He might do what you say.'

Maureen spoke as if she was whispering a secret.

'The Olsens won't break the chain. The way they says it is "don't break Momma's chain". Don't break Momma's chain. The sons has to keep on bein' Olsens, taking up the father's cause and if the father is wronged or the grandfather is wronged, the little boy has to carry on the cause forever. It's like the very same as if they're the king of England's son and has to be the prince even if they don't want to cos it's part of their duty and their breedin. And, Mo, there's no escapin' for us ader.'

Maureen didn't rightly know whose side she was on. She was always hoping Dermo would come good. Maybe that's what mothers are for. Everyone needs somebody who sees the good through the evil. But does that in some way give the bad son the impression that whatever he does, his mammy will still be there for him? It's not easy is it? Trying to figure out how to strike the right balance.

Maureen went on.

'Dermo died in the hospital, so your wishin' him dead is over. He went and died, so he did, and came back from the dead, so he did, and that means our Dermo's not going to die again no more, until he's old.'

Mo knew there and then Dermo learned of his death-wish escape from his mother.

'Don't mind the call and the hard ould talk,' continued Maureen. 'He don't mean none a dat. His ould head is still addled after the accident.'

Mo didn't reply. She didn't want to take away Maureen's sense of hope or her mother's dream of a rehabilitated Dermo. Maureen was always going on about how seemingly hopeless cases came good in the end. She prayed and prayed at her shrines. She prayed on her swollen, arthritic knees, through the terrible pain without any painkillers, for Dermo. Like an old saint living in a stone hut on an island who suffers so others will be forgiven. Maureen had been to the shrine at Knock seventeen times. She had great faith in Our Lady who was a mother. Our Lady and Dora Seerly would save her Dermo.

The problem was Maureen so believed in a happy outcome, she would fit Mo's silence into the fix as some sort of tacit acceptance there was hope for Dermo and Mo as a couple.

'If it's alright, can I stay over?' Maureen asked. 'I hate being on my own. Mikey is gone off on the lorry to Belgium for chocolate and burger mate.'

Mo was happy to have the company. She asked Maureen if she would make gravy with tomorrow's dinner.

'Can I ax you a favour?' asked Maureen.

Mo nodded.

'Course.'

'Take a peep down at me slippers.'

Maureen pulled both legs of her pink pyjama pants up to beyond her knees. Her tree trunk thighs were silky smooth. From there on down she was very hairy.

'I can't bend far enough with the old arthritis . . . to shave. It's being growin' for years and I'm too embarrassed to go to the beauty parlour in case they are all laughin' at me.'

Mo pulled up her sleeves.

'I'll be your beautician,' volunteered Mo.

She squirted the last of Dermo's shaving foam on Maureen's calves and shins. As Mo was shaving away, Maureen said, 'Do ya know what he used to call me – Jimmy John – my hubby. Dermo's Da. Do ya know? No you don't. Ah God. Wait'll ya hear this wan, Mo. His romantic nickname for me when we was goin' well?'

Mo stopped shaving so as to concentrate on what Maureen was going to say.

'What, Maur? Go on tell me. I'm dyin' to know,' said Mo as she took the top of another of the pink disposable razors when the first one silted up.

'He used to call me his oul' Clydesdale.'

I got to thinking of Dad and the master class he gave us in the last few months before he died. I used to think, well, they had us, so now it's up to our parents to look after us. It was like, why didn't they just do their jobs? What was all the arguing about? Our parents should be happy together, for us.

I was lying in bed with Dad watching a football game on TV. It was always like this between us. There I was with his arm around me. We never quit on that when I grew up, unlike other Dads who seemed to think it would stop their sons from being manly. Dad was still cramming advice into me now that he had so little time left.

'G, you know why parents sometimes make such a mess out of bringing up kids, is because we had parents ourselves. It's not a job you can ever rightly master. Just tell the kids the truth, is about the best advice, when you're talking to them. If there's truth you feel you need to keep from your children keep it away, if you think it's best. Not for you, but for your children.'

I grew up a lot in those last few months. My maturing was rushed. I know there should have been more sinking-in time.

Dad never bossed the remote but this one time, in the last week of his life, he turned the TV down. There were tears in his eyes. 'Hey, G. How did I do as a Dad?' It was my Dad looking for his end of term report from me, his boy.

We knew this was one of our last big talks before the rest of the family came back into the room.

'Dad. you were great. You did mess up sometimes, a little bit, but I always knew you loved us and that was good enough for me.'

'Thanks old pal,' said Dad.

I always loved it when he called me old pal because he was my oldest and my first pal. I knew he meant every word because my Dad always told me the truth when he was talking to me. I always told him the truth when I was talking to him.

Mo and Dermo would've been fine, if they had a Dad like mine.

The fer-de-lance was an angry little snake.

Perhaps it was down to the fact he was only 1.2 metres in length and suffered from some sort of small snake inferiority complex. The biggest of the fer-de-lance can grow to nearly 4 metres.

We had something in common, that snake and I.

The man on the banana plantation in St Lucia was angry too.

His beautiful wife had run off with an American tourist. The cheated husband threw the mad snake from a moist cloth sack into the banana box and sealed it several times over in strong plastic wrapping. The angry man thought for a second and, mindful of the snake's welfare on such a long journey, he pierced the wrapping several times with a knitting needle. Or maybe it was a pointy knife, as you would imagine there wouldn't be much call for jumpers in the heat of St Lucia.

The angry man would have his revenge even if the odds of killing the American who stole his wife was a billion, billion to one. The snake smuggler didn't even know if the wife stealer liked bananas, but someone somewhere would suffer.

Maybe that was how it happened. Who knows, but what we do know for certain is there was an angry fer-de-lance in the banana box exported from St Lucia.

Mo was in the newsagents. She glanced downwards at the paper.

It was page one. The headline caught her attention. SNAKE KILLS SOCIALITE. Mo read the story standing up.

The socialite died within seconds. She had already died socially. Her husband, who was nicknamed 3.4, was broke. He was given the handle 3.4, the paper said, because back in the boom, he was in the newspapers for buying this plot for 3.4 million and that house for 6.3 million and so on.

3.4 owed the banks 397 million. Lent for a development in Greece, which is even more broke than Ireland. And another mad scheme in some mountain ski resort in a remote part of Bulgaria where it only snowed diarrhoea snow for a month a year and was within a few hundred kilometres of a nuclear power plant with a slow puncture.

The dead lady had never been to a bargain supermarket before. It was in Hendon. In England. She and her husband had personally guaranteed all of their loans. Now they had to eat pasta in sauce out of a tin. The dead lady and her husband moved to the UK as bankruptcy tourists. The English laws were easier on the broke.

The cheap supermarkets never take the bananas out of the boxes. To spare money.

The lady grabbed a bunch on special offer. The bargain wasn't such a good deal. There was a free snake with every bunch. The fer-de-lance bit the bankrupt lady.

Thousands of fer-de-lance squirm at night on the roads of St Lucia, so much so the cars go bumpetty-bump as if they were being slowed down by speed ramps in a suburban rat run.

But there were no fer-de-lances lying on the roads in

Hendon and so there was panic.

The snake was chopped in two by a butcher. The tail-end was still wriggling. One-legged 'Hero Gran Hilda' battered the tail end of the dead snake with her crutch. She was brave, the papers reported, and resourceful too. Hilda removed the rubber bit from the end of the crutch with her false leg, and impaled the fer-de-lance on the supermarket floor until the police arrived.

But in the confusion and blood lust for the killing of the demonic serpent, the bankruptcy tourist was left writhing on the floor. She died, it seems, not from poison but from a heart attack, no more than a few metres away from a defibrillator hidden behind half-price Aloe Vera plants and ski wear for keeping out the cold on the pistes of Hendon.

The dead and only slightly poisoned woman was identified as Sorcha Mabelson.

The very same Sorcha Mabelson who told the school Mo was wearing her hand-me-down uniform in Clandeboyce.

Mo called to tell me the news and she was very distraught. Definitely she had wished Sorcha all the bad luck in the world, but that was ten years ago.

Mo was sobbing softly.

I promised to go see her the very next day. I had to. I couldn't bear it when Mo was crying.

The Dobermans were staring at me.

They were now fully grown now and had been moved out of the runs to a temporary holding area where they would be collected by North Koreans for use as gulag guard dogs and dissident eating.

This was the last time I would ever visit this place, or at least that was the way I looked at it back then. I was there for Mo, not me. A mission of mercy to help her recover from the shock of the fer-de-lance killing of Sorcha Mabelson, or so I convinced myself.

The dogs were barking like mad. I stopped for a second to take a look at the hounds. They were huge now. Bigger than their mother.

I put my hands on the wire and called the dogs over. 'Here, boy. Here, boy,' and I made spittle klich sounds by pushing my tongue up against a grinder.

I barked at the dogs just to get them going.

The Dobermans went completely crazy.

The second Doberman came from out of my eye line and snapped at me through the fence, almost biting my fingers off. The smaller hound charged at the wire and then tried to climb over but he couldn't get a paw hold on the narrow diamonds in the fence.

The dogs' ears had been cut and the stumps were standing up. Dermo did the cutting, because it made the Dobermans look more ferocious. Floppy ears were droopy which maybe had some connection in Dermo's mind with impotence.

I stood and watched the fury.

Saliva dripped from their mouths. The dogs' eyes were all white. The barking was loud and didn't stop even for a second.

I couldn't believe how high they could jump but then again I should have remembered the hanging rabbit in the runs. The bigger dog leapt almost horizontally from his powerful hind legs, catching his paws on the very top of the fence, almost pulling it down with the force of his body weight.

His pads were scratched and bleeding from the sharp, thorn-shaped steel ends on top of the fence.

The dogs must have weighed about seventy kilos each. Their thrust carried a force of three times that of a human. The dog equivalent of six rugby players were crash-tackling the wire fence. The fence began to shake and then slacken. It hadn't been attached to concrete poles in a sound foundation, which was standard practice. The Olsens didn't do standard practice. The fence was nailed onto a shaky lean-to shed on one side and was tied by wire cable to a timber electricity pole. The once taut fence was now slack on the shed side end and the dogs concentrated their efforts there.

I walked quickly towards the house, anxiously looking back.

The fence was slackening with every jump but I still felt safe enough as the house was only about 150 metres away, at the far end of the Compound.

One of the dogs became hopelessly entangled in the wire and his fish-in-a-net frenzy weakened the fence even further from the base up. The horseshoe-shaped nails holding down the fence were coming up out of the cement yard.

Now there was a danger the dogs could escape under the wire.

I ran. But I was slow as I was wearing my new heel-for-height patent leather shoes with shiny slippery soles of silky leather.

The smallest Doberman piggybacked on his pal and jumped out over the half-fallen fence on to the other side. I ran as fast as I could.

I slipped on grease or oil. The mad dog was gaining ground. He ran like a greyhound. His big shoulders pumping, his muscled neck sticking out and his head looking straight ahead, fully focused on his target.

I fell again, like a drunk, on the wet decking in front of the porch.

Mo dragged me along the decking. The dog stopped for a second when one of my shoes fell off and he snapped it in his mouth, most probably having mistaken if for my leg. That slight delay saved me.

She barely got me in the door and slammed it shut, almost catching the Doberman's snotty snout. The dog was jumping at the door. Trying to knock it down. Every jump was a thud. Mo pulled across the bolts Mikey put in to keep Dermo out.

'Jesus, what happened?' asked Mo, out of breath. 'They're going nuts.'

By now the second dog freed himself from the wire tangle and the two were laying siege to the door, jumping at it in turns.

Mo had left the living room window open. The first Doberman spotted the weakness in the fortifications and jumped at the window but he too slipped on the wet decking surrounding the house. For a few seconds the dog was winded and disorientated. I hobbled to the window, as one leg was shorter than the other because of the missing shoe, and slammed the window closed. The dog got back on his feet and jumped at the pane of glass without any consideration for his own safety.

The force of the Doberman's attack left a hair crack on the double glazed window.

The dogs scratched the paint off the front door through the mesh. After a few minutes, the Dobermans gave up trying to huff and puff and blow the house down.

'My heart, it's pounding. I thought you were finished.'

Mo took time to get her breath back.

'I . . . I heard the barking and I rushed out of the shower. I just had a feeling you were in trouble. You got here early – it was just so lucky that I opened the bathroom window. I barely heard the barking above the water.'

She was flushed from the terror of the dogs as she sat beside me in a black and red silk kimono.

'Oh God, if something happened to you.'

She made tea with sugar for the shock.

Long, wet tangled ringlets fell down like catkins on her breasts and printed her erect nipples through the kimono. Her knees and a little above to her thigh showed her long brown legs.

Mo stroked the tips of her fingers gently and slowly across my forehead.

'Come on,' I said, 'I need a big hug.'

'Keep the hug. I'm so horny.' And she pushed her pelvis into my face.

I didn't respond, because, well because I didn't know how to respond.

Mo sat beside me on the couch. Her face was pale now.

'So sorry, G. I'm so embarrassed.'

'No. No it's okay. Don't be. I've always wanted you, Mo but I was afraid if I told you I loved you, it would end our friendship.'

Mo waited for a second and loosened the silk belt but somehow the Kimono stayed closed.

'I was thinking of . . . you when I was in the shower.' In that slow, low hoarse voice.

'Oh, Mo if you only knew how many million wanks I dedicated to you.'

We kissed.

The silk kimono opened like curtains. I saw all of her naked. The beauty of her, the raunchiness.

I sort of felt duty bound to ask, even though I wanted her there and then. But I had to say it, out of politeness.

'Will I do foreplay?' as she masturbated silently before me, watching my every expression.

'Just pull across the curtains. That's all the foreplay I need.'

I jumped up, grabbed the curtains and pulled so hard the one on the left came off the tracks. There was no sign of the Dobermans.

'Do it to me now.'

I was unbuckling my belt.

'Are you sure about the foreplay?'

Mo pulled me to her.

'We've had five years of that.'

We made love, at last.

There was no going away from her now.

It was meant to be from the first time we met in the club.

The ideas came quickly. Dermo would be in the hospital for another month at least. She had to be out of the Compound before his return. The city was too near the Olsens. Everywhere in Ireland was too near the Olsens. We decided it was Oz. The twins were settled and the Australians were looking for guys like me down in Perth where the mining boom was still in progress. Mo would go back to college in Australia and finish her degree.

Mo asked what would happen to my mother, who would be on her own with all her kids far away in Australia, and we started to plan all over again.

Tough decisions were going to have to be made.

For all her bravery and women's groups, my mother hated being on her own. My mother needed someone to boss. My mother had to be busy.

There was leaving Maureen. There was leaving Ireland. Leaving Ireland didn't bother Mo, but leaving Maureen did. We made love again. This time in a bed. Not the marital bed but in the spare room, in the candlelight. Slowly. Mo gave a master class.

My car was marooned in the middle of the Compound. It was dark now. Mo warned I had better be out of there before Maureen came home from the city.

It seemed as if the dogs were well gone. Mo would call the cops when I left. Tell them the Dobermans had escaped, and were dangerous and armed. The Compound was as quiet as it had ever been. Mo drove me over to my car just in case the dogs were hiding out, ready to pounce.

'That was the first time I ever made love to a man I truly loved,' she said holding my hand, as we sat in the car making our goodbyes, and setting up our next move.

'I suppose,' I said, 'we always loved each other.'

We kissed.

'Did you know, G, you're a very gentle type of person?'

We checked again for Dobermans.

I howled like a wolf out of the window of the car. I had seen just how fast they were, and thought it might be as well to flush them out. We waited silently, listening, in the car, with the windows half open and the doors locked.

Mo kissed me goodbye.

The back door of my car was still open. There was a commotion but it was only a pigeon clattering and cooing out of one of the sheds.

I back-heeled the door closed without looking behind me, still scanning the Compound out in front.

I didn't know why, but I just couldn't savour the day for the whole way home.

I had a sense this was all too big for me. Now that we were going to be together forever. There would be kids.

We might have to go to Oz. Live there for the rest of our lives. For our own safety.

All this was happening too fast and too unplanned, for me, who worked at making sketches and measurements of buildings, each of which was strictly adhered to and validated by the clients and the planning authority.

How was Mam going to work Skype without me? My mother couldn't even figure in which direction to point the TV zapper.

There was a full moon and it seemed to follow the car as I drove along. It was the same old moon that lit us all the way home when Dad drove back from the big football games in Dublin.

Most of my serious thinking is done in the bubble of the car. It goes back to school days when we used to say our prayers in Dad's old Escort.

'I'm the only Dad in the school who shifts a twenty-two-year-old Escort every day.' He was always joking and I always laughed. Dad was very funny.

Dad an' me. That was our quality time. Mam was always interrupting when we were on our own at home. It was if she was checking up on what he was saying to me. Censoring his talking in case I turned out like him.

Then, as I thought it all through in the analysis after ecstasy, it was as if that pivotal moment when I made love to the woman of my dreams was the end of the carefree student and first job days.

Here I was all grown up, ready to have kids of my own and me just a few years out of adolescence. It was like the time I said to Dad when I was a kid that the white sliced sandwich bread was all dirty. He explained when the bakers changed from making brown bread to white, some of the brown flour was still in the machine and it blended into the white sliced pan. That was me. In between a boy and a man with bits of each in the mix.

It was scary and exciting all at the same time. Mo was dying for a kid. I was certain she would be the best mother ever. All that woman ever wanted was a happy home with babies, to make up in some way for the one who died inside her. To make up for her own lost childhood.

She said I was cute. I was dapper. I always knew that. Possibly I was the only one of the boys, here at home or gone away, who owned a dentist's mirror. Every morning I checked if there were rogue hairs sticking out of me, like the old men with enough wax in their ears to grow spuds in.

The windscreen started to fog up. I thought of the dogs and worried they might attack someone. A movie clip came into my head. A real one this time, from an actual movie. There was a mad dog hiding in the back of car, in the film, and when the driver looked in the mirror there was the mad dog staring at him.

I was singing this song I used to sing for Mo, for laughs. It was a parody of Caledonia

> *Oh let me tell you that I love me*
> *And I dream about me all the time*
> *Tommy G I love you*
> *And I'm goin' home*

There was an erotic flashback to when Mo placed her finger underneath me.

'That's the way I do it to myself when I'm thinking

about you,' she sighed hoarsely, as she licked and gently held and bit my nipples.

I felt a sudden extreme unstoppable spontaneous sensuous pleasure move me to an immediate road safety hazard of a hard erection. There should be penalty points for driving with an erection, I thought. The temptation was to head back to the Compound and risk death and mutilation. It went through my head that if I crashed the coroner would console my loved ones with an 'At least he died happy.'

Very much in love with myself, I looked in the mirror.

The sad-eyed Doberman seemed calm enough. As if he was a family pet out for a drive in the country. He had the resigned aura of a Buddhist monk who came back to earth as a dog. The erection melted as quickly as snow in the Sahara. The Law of the Wish struck again. 'Thinking brings being.'

He saw me looking at him and I saw him looking at me. There wasn't a bark or a word between us. The huge dog took up the whole of the central inside mirror like he was filling up a canvass. But I did see the dog's flanks in the twisted left wing mirror. He was torn to pieces.

The dog lunged and bit my ear off. I have large enough ears and I suppose the one on the left, nearer the passenger seat, was less protected and presented an easier target. Blood pumped out and I crashed into a ditch but not fatally. Well I wouldn't be writing this would I, if I was killed. No one writes books posthumously.

The Doberman must have been bollixed from his injuries. He just couldn't get up and at me a second time. I managed to get out of the car, this time remembering to close the door, and to bring my mobile phone, but I forgot my ear. I called 999. The lady who answered seemed so calm. I was already mentally deranged.

She asked, 'Where did it happen?'

'Where do you think?' I answered somewhat annoyed at her lack of professionalism.

'Behind my head, opposite my other ear,' stating the obvious.

The nurse from the hospital was on her way home from the 2 to 10 shift. The Doberman was barking like crazy and was looking out the window at me. The back window began to fog up from his breath. Calm as could be, as if it was an everyday occurrence, the nurse asked, 'Where is your ear?

'Which one?' I asked.

'The one that's missing.'

'In the car,' I said, bleeding but not as badly as you might think.

I was completely nuts by now from the shock.

'I have to phone the lads in Oz. Jeeez they'll never believe this one.'

The nurse looked in the window and the Doberman was still there, it being a well-known fact Dobermans can't open car doors or kick them out from inside. Although in light of the break-out from the Compound, I wouldn't put it past them.

'Is he your dog?'

'I don't even know if he's a he. Has he a willy?

The nurse asked me again.

'Is he yours?'

'No, I just gave him a lift.'

By now she must have guessed I was gone loopy. The nurse opened the door of the car and the injured dog, revived from a rest and juiced up with adrenalin, jumped up at her. He took a bite out of the headrest, which must have had a smell of me off it.

The nurse found my ear on the front seat and managed to grab it quickly while the Doberman was trying to get through the gap between the driver seat and the passenger seat, but he was too big and he was too badly injured.

She got me into her car and put my ear in between a bag of frozen American Collection Buffalo Wings and Bird's Eye peas. She was the one and the same nurse who saved Dermo. Dora would surely write about it all when Maureen let her in on the series of events.

'Don't go cooking my ear,' I ordered.

'Don't worry. I'm not that hungry.'

We were in A&E within ten minutes. It was full of the maimed, the half-dead, the infirm and those with fuck all wrong with them.

It's amazing how quickly you can get through the queues when your ear is bitten off.

'Come with me, Van Gogh,' requested the junior doctor, and less than hour later the ear was sewn back on by a plastic surgeon.

In the end, the Doberman choked to death, on car-seat upholstery foam.

The Olsens were devastated. It was like 'a death in the family' was how Mikey put it. The Alsatians met the Dobermans in the Compound and they fought to the end. Grey couldn't be found. It was thought he was dead in some ditch. 'He must've crawled off and died,' said a broken-hearted Mikey.

Mo cried for Grey. 'He was a gentleman.'

Bit by bit I began to recover. The hospital routine was boring and the nurse's take on it was, 'When you notice you're getting bored, you are getting better.'

The boredom left when I had a visit from the police.

It was the one and only Sergeant Matt. On his own.

My mother was visiting when Matt called. Mam came up to the city with one of the neighbours from Bally. He did the driving as Mam wasn't used to the traffic in the city. Tim was a friend of Dad's and he was very good to us after Dad died. He was a retired cop and pulled the twins out of a dope rap when the stupid little goms were caught passing a joint around at mass on Palm Sunday.

It seems they had been at it for a while and lit up every Sunday when the priest started swinging the thurible, giving off a lovely smokey smell of burnt Middle Eastern incense, which masked the fumes from the hash.

Big Matt puffed up and got straight down to business.

'Tell Big Matt what conspired on the night of the twenty-seventh ultimo. Let me tell you firstly young man the deceased dog was found in a terrible condition in your car. The poor creature died a cruel death, alone and choking, so far away from those who love him. He has no one to speak for him so therefore Big Matt will do his talking for him. By Jove he will. Big Matt will be the canine's advocate.'

He lowered his head in sympathy.

'Now, young man, where did the canine in question come from?'

'What?'

'Where did the dog come from?'

'Mammy and daddy dogs,' I replied. 'Like all doggies.'

Big Matt bristled. Out went his chest but he failed to pull in his belly.

'Now young man—'

My mother jumped to my defence before Matt could make another speech.

'What are you saying? Are you saying my son deliberately attacked a dog? Why should he do such a thing? He's in here now in a bad way after having his ear bitten off by a mad hound and here you are, in here, in a hospital, interrogating him. He could have rabies you know.'

Big Matt didn't try to put a gloss on it.

'We are only making enquiries, Madame. And to put your mind at ease there is no rabies in Ireland. To my certain knowledge. Beyond a reasonable doubt and beyond that doubt too. Beyond even an unreasonable doubt. If there was rabies in Ireland Big Matt would know it, Madame. Be sure, be very sure. If a man sneezes with hay fever, Big Matt knows it. It's Big Matt's business to know things,' declared Matt, knowingly.

My mother, who had been sitting on the edge of my bed, stood up and faced the Supercop. Mam was brave.

'I have friends in the media you know and I have the ear of the people. How dare you insinuate my son had anything to do with that mongrel's death, and stop calling me Madame like I was a receptionist in a whorehouse.'

Matt backed off as if to have a better look at Mam.

Timmy asked Matt out for a private word.

'In a minute, in a minute, sir,' said Matt angrily.

Big Matt took several photographs from a large envelope and threw them on the bed, one by one, like he was dealing cards.

The Doberman was in a desperate condition with bones protruding through his black and tan crew-cut coat. The dog's tongue was sticking out of the side of his mouth.

'The dog suffered beyond endurance. What sir, do you know of this?'

Timmy let it be known, he too was 'a member'. Big Matt left with Timmy and we could see them chatting and laughing outside the door of my room through the glass peep-in.

I had the feeling Big Matt's subsequent interrogation

was all for show. At no stage did he press me on the ownership of the dogs. He knew who owned the dead Doberman. He had to. Matt couldn't have cared less about the dead dog. He was snooping.

I recited an Oliver Goldsmith poem we learned by heart at school.

The wound it seemed both sore and sad
To every Christian eye;
And while they swore the dog was mad,
They swore the man would die.

But soon a wonder came to light,
That showed the rogues they lied:
The man recovered of the bite,
The dog it was that died.

'Capital,' critiqued Big Matt. 'Excellent. Big Matt loves a chuckle. Young man you have a rare talent. BM knows his oats when it comes to poetry and that poem you have written is poetry with a capitol P, if I may say so.'

Big Matt said he knew for sure we were wonderful, decent honest people. Apologies to my mother for calling her Madame, 'Which in the context it was used in was no more than a form of address used ad infinitum in France and polite circles in Ireland.'

My mother was not for appeasement.

'My son is in a bad way and here ye are torturing him over a hyena of a dog that bit his ear off. My son left his car door open for a minute when he went out to check the tyres, the dog snuck in. It would be more in your line to find out who owns the dogs instead of going after an innocent boy still recovering after a major operation.'

Big Matt left without any parting words.

Timmy was calm. 'Mary, don't be getting upset now. He's alright is Matt. That'll be the end of it. Someone had to check the owner of the car. That's it now. It's over and the less fuss, the better.'

Timmy was calling my mother Mary and then it dawned on me, I hardly knew her first name. She was always just Mam or Mammy.

Big Matt was on a reconnaissance mission. He needed to suss me out and find out how much I knew about him and his connection with the Olsens.

My mother was all questions about the ear but I told her it was fine. She too liked to know things.

The truth was an ear nerve had been severed and the doctors said it could take up to a year to repair itself. Even then there was no guarantee. Nerves take months to grow back. Less than a millimetre a day and there was no certainty the nerves would connect into the nerves on the other side of the divide.

Mo spent hours with me in the hospital, yet every hour was like a minute. I was still in terrible pain. My hair was flat on the good ear side as I couldn't sleep on the other side. Much as I tried to fluff it up, it never really matched. Funny isn't it, the consequences of unexpected acts. Bet Van Gogh didn't think his hair would be spoiled when he was trying to impress the hooker. I'll bet he didn't paint too many sunflowers after he chopped his ear off either. I bet if he gave her a fifty, it would have sweetened her up a lot more. Self-mutilation is fine if your leg is stuck in a crevice on a high mountain and you're out of phone range or credit and the only way to survive is to hack it off with a pen knife, but aside from that it's not to be recommended.

Every day, when the nurses and the helpers were finished their check-ups and feeding and blood samples, Mo slipped her hand under the stiff sheets.

During that holistic treatment I experienced no pain, which is kind of weird, which goes to show if you could get a tablet that replicated the pleasure from a hand job, then there would be an end to suffering, for men anyway, with Nobel prizes for medicine and millions from the drug companies. Bet there would be no shortage of takers for the clinical trials.

The occupational therapist told me I had to train my ear nerves into accepting touch. She spoke of the nerves as if they were a different person to the rest of my body.

'They have become used to not being touched and you must now change the way they think. It's a gradual thing. First we use the cotton wool. Then we will massage the ear very gently with moisturising cream for two minutes, gradually building up the time and the pressure used in the massage.'

Mo rubbed the cream on my ear. But the pain was so bad I cried.

'G, I love you so much and I never want to be away from you again.'

I told her I loved her too and life would be very boring without her.

The plan was to get me out of the hospital as soon as possible. There was a risk of infection and the surgeon warned me that the ' MSRI bug is killing more patients than us doctors.'

I was well treated though. Nurses are saints. They were

lovely to me and my Mam was given tea and biscuits. She loved that and I loved her, even though there were times she would drive you nuts.

Her standing up to the forces of justice reminded me just how tough she could be. My mother would be able to withstand anything life threw at her. If we left for Oz though she would be heartbroken. Mam always wanted the best for us and that was her reason for living. She didn't rear us for export, but she had to be aware that economic life here is a cycle.

Stop me if you've heard this one, or skip a few lines. Texting has killed the joke. It's impossible to get one that hasn't been sent to thousands in only a few minutes. It's an old Irish mother gag. Sort of sums up my mother but in another way it doesn't tell the full story. Mothers will moan but they have an infinite capacity to get on with life. They know well kids must make their own mistakes and make their own lives but mothers can't help directing. I suppose if you've had someone swimming around inside of you for nine months, you'd be slow enough to let the kids swim without those arm floats too.

I'm sure we had a great old time in the womb. It's a heated kiddies pool and a spa too. With lots of splashing and swimming. The little ones spend their day gurgling happy songs, on a lead.

Anyway, sorry and all that if you've heard the gag before. Nothing worse than some boring bollix regurgitating jokes you've heard time and time again.

Okay.

Question:

How many Irish mothers does it take to change a light bulb?

Answer:

None. I'll just sit here in the dark all by myself.

Like I say there were times when I used to wanna throw momma from the train.

I told her about Mo and me. I had to. I sorta figured telling her while I was lying here in the hospital bed in agony and totally traumatised, might soften the blow. I mean, you couldn't give out to a man who had his ear bitten off in a totally random and unprovoked Doberman attack.

My mother didn't say anything for a second or two.

'I thought she was married?'

Her arms were folded now.

'Separated.'

Mother didn't do hesitation when she had a witness in the box.

'Are ye movin in together?'

'Fairly soon. I'd say. Like as in next week.'

'Right. You'll be moving out of home so.'

'I was sort of hoping we could stay with you for a while until we got sorted out with our own place.'

My mother was at her most maternal when you gave in. There was a softness there but it only surfaced when you were really shagged, like as in having your ear ripped off or after a blow-up, when she knew she had gone too far with her temper and criticism.

'I'll never refuse my own son a bed in his own home.'

The only way through her was to get round her.

'Don't worry Mam, we'll take separate beds and all that.

Mo can sleep in the twins' room.'

Mam the liberal spoke up.

'Sure ye might as well sleep together as you're at it. Sure won't ye be in the one bed when ye get your own place. It's a temporary arrangement, mind. For a few months. At most. I'll help you, financially, to rent your own place. If you don't get work. The radio want me to do the show five days a week now.'

Like I say, mothers can get used to anything. I was surprised. Mam wanted a woman for me from my own social background. The father of her ideal partner for me might be a teacher and the mother a retired teacher, who gave up her job to look after the kids. There might be a bit of land and a holiday home on the seaside – all paid for. The daughter would have to be pretty but not beautiful. Mam advised the husbands' friends will always try to hit on wives who are too voluptuous.

'And I speak from experience.'

Dad's pals tried to hit on her. She made the announcement on *The Woman's Hour*. Dr Lucia Quinn-McManus maintained, 'Most Irish men think the clitoris is a perennial flower that thrives in sandy soil and shade.' Mam was now not only the first woman to say 'orgasm' on local radio but also the first to allow someone to say clitoris.

Maybe Mam just wanted me to be happy.

I was sitting on the edge of bed, staring out the window at the silver-grey roof of the hospital. Seagulls docked for a while before flying off in search of chippers and sloppy bin men. Junkie magpies picked resin and glue with their pointy black beaks from the joins in the aluminium roof.

Dermo was still there in St Hilda's. Just a few floors down. We were told his condition had deteriorated and he hardly knew his mother. With any luck, he would vegetate away the rest of his life in the home for the bewildered.

I didn't think I would be capable of killing him violently but if wishes could kill, he would be six feet under by now.

My awakemares had him sitting on a wheelchair, by an open window, with a vase of Van Gogh's sunflowers on the sill. Mo's face was in the middle of every flower and Dermo was bouncing my one-eared head up and down like it was a basketball.

Maureen told Mo he was pushing a Zimmer frame now. It beats me how Zimmer was such a frigging hero. He's world famous for inventing a piece of metal tubing you shove along the floor to stop yourself falling down. And he was loaded rich from the patent royalties. I mean it isn't exactly the zip or cats' eyes or a cure for cancer. Then some affiliate or associate comes up with another brainwave and makes billions more. They put wheels on it. Wheels, whoa. Imagine, sixty-three million centuries after Trog the caveman figured out stuff moves faster when you wheel it up, Zimmer's guys finally get the message.

I was always racking my brain for the big idea.

My buddies had visions of an internet start-up they would eventually sell for 124 million and it wouldn't even have even been hard work with everyone coming in to the office in baseball caps turned back to front and playing basketball into the net hanging over the bosses' desks to get ideas and everyone being caring to fellow workers and high fives and huge bonuses and toy trains running all over the office and cancelling Mondays and hugs and the bosses showing up at meetings with merchant bankers in sandals and surfer's shorts and hairy legs and two-day stubble and having staff think-ins at Electric Picnic.

It became a national obsession with us young guys when the bust came. Getting the big idea to take you out of here and into rich countries like China where the money was burning a hole in their pockets, just like it did to ours.

If the *DoZoPop* idea didn't work I had another plan.

The Irish are mad for funerals. We cash in on that. The Irish spend a fortune on coffins and even have horse-drawn hearses with men dressed in Charles Dickens black suits with high hats and black silk cummerbunds and white faces, even more deathly looking than their clients.

It beats me how it is undertakers were always so pale. Maybe they put on Factor 50 all year round to show empathy with their punters. I remember when my Dad died the undertaker looked so fucked, I was going to take the old man out of the coffin for a while so the funeral director could have a lie down.

That was the day I had the idea. He died at six in the morning. I was asleep on the floor beside his bed. The doctor told us he could go that night so we took turns staying up, but we dozed off, exhausted after several nights staying up minding Dad.

Mam woke us. 'He's breathing very fast and heavy. I think he's going to go.' We hustled the twins out of their bunk beds. The poor fellas were full of sleep and rubbed their eyes hard in unison.

'Come on twins hurry up. We have to say goodbye to Dad.'

'Why, where's he going?' asked Al.

'Heaven'

'Is he going to die?'

'Yeah probably.'

'But he is going to heaven?'

'For sure. Yeah. Guaranteed.'

The twins were too tired to cry, too young to see their Dad die. I was too young to see my Dad die. I needed him for a good few more years, just as I need him now.

The day before he died I met up with Mame Moran in our local shop. O'Brien's was a real shop with shovels for sale beside underpants, no three-for-the-price-of-two useless things the hypermarkets couldn't sell or unethical prawns in satay, or crap you didn't need. It was nearly out of date packets of biscuits, tins of pears, cream paint and the just hanging on to their business and being deadly nice to everyone and not only for the money. Everything tastes different in O'Brien's.

I thought Dad might be able to eat baby food and bought a couple of small bottles of mashed-up vegetables or some such shite they make the babies eat.

Mame sensed what I was thinking.

'For your dad?'

'Yeah.'

'Is he in pain?'

'Yeah Mame. Not too bad, but sort of bad enough at the same time. He's on stuff. For the pain. But he wants to go off it. So he knows what's goin' on.'

'I hope you don't mind me saying this but he'll

know when it's time to go, G.'

I was listening carefully because Mame was a smart woman. I knew what she was telling me felt right.

'I often sit up with the neighbours. The ones who have no one when they are dying or if someone needs a break if they are too tired. They're hanging on for dear life but most in pain want to go. They have to be told, it's okay to take their leave. Your Dad is mad about you. He'll know it's you, even if he is very bad, and only barely conscious. Tell him, G. Tell him and he will understand.'

He came round a bit later that day and even ate a spoon or two of the baby food.

The four of us were by the bed.

'Dad, you'll be fine,' I said.

'You were always a desperate bad liar.'

'We're all here with you, Dad'

His long greying hair was flat and limp where there had been curls. I squeezed his hand and he summoned up enough strength to squeeze back. We kissed him. Our Dad who kissed his boys like he was a friggin' Italian or something. Our Dad who was the only Dad around the village who kissed his sons.

Mam was on the other side of the bed. She didn't hold his hand but she did nurse him through the last few months with absolute efficiency.

The twins were silent. Even Al, the talking twin. Their spokesman, Dad called him. They were well old enough to know what was going on but I think there some sort of tacit acceptance it was my job as the oldest to send him on his way, even though the truth was I was no more than a boy myself.

I took on the responsibility. I didn't want Mam and the lads to hear for fear they wouldn't understand what was going on between us.

I whispered in his ear again. 'You can go now, Dad. We're all here with you. Mam and me and the twins.'

It took him a few minutes to shut down. He gave out a few last breaths and he died with all his family there beside him.

We stayed in the room for a while without speaking. A ray of light came in the bedroom window and shone like a spot on a photograph of Dad. He was smiling in the photograph and I, in my emotional and exhausted state, thought he was actually alive in the frame telling us he was okay. Sometimes though I think it really was a sign but I never told anyone except Mo, who didn't take much notice after all she had heard about death from Maureen and accepted what I was telling her as normal. But there was something going on out there in the vastness or smallness of wherever it is we go when we die.

There I was sitting on my bed, dressed up for the road home with my ear bandaged up like a work of art before it's unveiled, thinking of the old man's death, in a hospital where there probably four or five people ready to breathe their last that very day. I felt so small and powerless up against the vastness and scale of all that was going on in the world. The world is too big. I'm too small.

Mam and Mo were coming to get me.

It was good to be going home, even if I was in pain. Good to get back to visiting my Dad up at the grave. Good to get out of the hospital where they woke you for breakfast at seven and lunch was served at twelve, which was breakfast time for me after I lost my job. Good to get back to hisbrotherwasworse.ie.

hisbrotherwasworse.ie would make me rich. The big idea. And I was thinking of another less quirky name like sorryforyourtroubles.ie, which was the standard line when you met the bereaved.

hisbrotherwasworse.ie came from a story the old fella told me. I think he got it from a DVD made by the actor Eamon Kelly. Dad kept on playing it until he had every word off by heart.

It goes like this and it happens at the funeral of this truly horrible and deeply unpopular dude. No one can think of anything good to say about him. Back in the old days it was the custom to praise the dead, even if you cut the livin' shite out of them when they were alive.

The funeral goers scratched their heads and went through the back catalogue of the dead man's deeds, but not a good word could be found in praise of the deceased. Then one of the gang at the funeral comes out with the best eulogy he can manage: 'His brother was worse.' And that's where we got the name.

I had been in touch with a web designer and a couple of buddies who were journalists and couldn't get work. The orders for obituaries would roll in from all over Ireland and then the world. There would be ads on the site for undertakers and whoever was working in the death business like embalmers, ambulance-chasing lawyers, mass card printers, florists, bereavement counsellors, headstone sculptors, grave diggers, dating agencies and mediums.

The loved ones would be praised and made blessed.

'Our darling Dad was loved by one and all. He was a generous man. Dad killed a ram every Christmas and gave his nuts to the poor.'

We were going to publish and write all the obits on hisbrotherwasworse.ie.

Then we would set up a page like Facebook for the dead. A book of condolences. Like the Egyptians, with drawings and wise words. There would be little tributes by people who couldn't make the funeral and a MyPics of the deceased with links to anything he did on YouTube. That sort of thing.

We couldn't lose. When I say we, I mean Mo and me. She was in for 50:50, even though it was all my idea, but that was the way it was going to be from now on. Halves in everything including and especially our baby, when the time was right.

The banks wouldn't lend us a cent. The manager decided it was too high-risk.

He tapped a pencil on his desk as he told us the bad news.

It drove me nuts.

Then he stopped tapping and asked, 'Anything else?' Which really meant your time is up, now get outta here. Five years earlier they would have given us ten million and ask have you enough in that?

'Do you have any rubbers ?' Mo asked before we left.

'Rubbers?' asked the thrown bank manager.

'Yeah,' said Mo, 'for the bottom of your pencil.' He was lucky she left at that and didn't wish him dead.

Mam and Mo hooked up and came to the hospital

together. My mother fussed over me while Mo looked on quietly, afraid my Mam would say something that would hurt her. It was a bit like when the old boss is still clearing her desk and the new boss is waiting on her to move out. My mother interrogated Mo in the car on the way to the hospital. Asked her about the status of her divorce and how would she pay her way if she didn't have any money and what if any were her job prospects and there was always McDonald's.

Mo carried my bag and Mam took my laptop.

The hospital was really busy. The entrance narrowed into a bottleneck, at the point where the coffee shop and the bustling reception area intersected.

He didn't seem to notice us at first. Dermo had lost a lot of weight and his eyes were grey. It looked as if the mad squatters in his head had left for another host.

It was pretty shocking for Mo. After all, she was married to him. You would just have to feel for him and then again you wouldn't.

Dermo's nurse took the wrapping off a bar of chocolate. Dermo broke off a piece. We stood and watched from behind a large pillar, without which the hospital would have fallen down. Every now and then our view of him was blocked by passersby. A hospital helper sneezed three billion molecules of deadly germs into the air. Two one-legged men passed each other in the corridor without so much as a hello. A lost young girl who looked to be about thirteen months' pregnant looked up at the signs for directions to the wards, here in the very hospital where Mo lost her baby.

Dermo blinked several times. He sneezed and wiped his

nose with his sleeve. The sneezing started up again and with such violence Dermo's head recoiled each time in a whiplash movement. The nurse cleaned his nose and face. Dermo looked up over the cloth as if he were peeping over the top of a yashmak.

He threw himself from the wheelchair when he saw Mo peeping out from behind the pillar. Dermo crawled quickly across the floor in our direction.

'You tried to kill me with a hammer. Your poor husband what is only ever mindin' everyone. A man what never done nottin to no wan.'

Mo ran.

The nurse picked up a kicking and revolving Dermo with the help of a security man who wheeled him away.

'You're all dead. Dead. I swear to God. Dead fucking dead, dead, dead. I swear to God I'll get ye.'

'You, you!' he screamed at me. 'She's my wife. Mine. Give her back. You fucking wife robber you!'

His voice trailed off as he was pushed into a lift at the end of the corridor. Mo had to sit down. My mother got her a drink of water and rubbed her hands. Mo was shaking. Her face was pale and her legs were so weak she couldn't stand up. I put my arms around Mo and told her I would always mind her.

Maureen said she would die of loneliness if Mo left.

Mo was adamant she was going to leave and soon. As it was, there was no danger from Dermo who was wheelchair-bound for now, and would be sent to prison for four years, or even more according to Timmy. Our Garda family friend.

Maureen asked Mo to give up her marital property claim to the Compound in favour of Dermo. Maureen was sure Dermo would need constant care 'near his old mammy, when he was wished better, or came out of the hospital, and the prison, eventually.' Mo was relieved in that she saw the signing over as part of the process of leaving her husband.

'I just want to be shut of him forever.'

Maureen was sure Dermo would be less likely to look for revenge if Mo signed the house over. And then she corrected herself quickly by saying, 'That's if he ever do come around to his full senses.'

'Ah but he's very bad and maybe someday when he do get better and I'm sure he will, God willing, ye might be friends again when he's back to hisself. With the help of God and his blessed mother.' Maureen was truly beginning to annoy her.

The solicitors took a while to sort out the paperwork for the transfer of Mo's share of the house. Then there was Maureen's sixtieth, which took up another week. Maureen was trying her best to cling on to Mo for as long as possible.

Maureen issued almost daily bulletins on Dermo's progress.

'He's not able to speak too well after the three mini-strokes but theys giving him speaking therapy. Teachin' him to talk all over agin the poor cratur. The angry things weren't him at all. All the doctors said that. Even the foreign wans. It was the accident. He ate shepherd's pie today.' Probably with a shepherd in it.

In the end Mo told Maureen, crossly, she didn't want to hear another word about Dermo, and she didn't care if she ever saw him again. About a week before Mo was due to leave, Maureen, as a treat, purchased a sixtieth present for herself, and a goodbye to the Compound present for Mo. It was a surprise trip to the Canaries

Mo refused the holiday but she gave in when Maureen showed her the brochures. It was cold for early spring and the bitter north-east wind blew through the Compound for days on end. Mo longed for sun and blue light.

The hotel was on Gran Canaria. A themed African village with tall, thatched huts and an azure lagoon.

'It's a girl's trip. Tanning, shopping, cocktails. That sort of thing.'

Maureen was now resigned to Mo's leaving the Compound for good.

'I'm sorry about trying to fix up you and Dermo. It's just that I love you like the daughter I never had.'

There were floods of tears. Mo painted Maureen's bitten finger nails. Mo said Maureen's nails were like little islands surrounded by acres of rosy flesh.

'Trip of a lifetime. I'll be like a cooked chicken when I come back. The white meat will be the best,' said Mo, who couldn't wait for the holiday. She was never anywhere farther away from her flat than one of the seaside towns near the city and only then for a day out. It was her first plane trip. I was happy for Mo and Maureen too.

We made love on the night before she left, several times, 'Just in case I get tempted over there. You know what Irish girls are like on their holliers.'

Irish women, around my age and younger, went a bit on the wild side when they went away on holidays. Most of the girls didn't see sex as any big deal. Especially on holiday. I trusted Mo but when it came to sex, she just didn't take it seriously enough. 'It's only natural,' she said, 'and anything natural is good.'

One night we were out for an American ride, in the car, and she said something that stuck in my mind when we pulled in to a lay-by, for the real ride.

'I think like a man.'

I wasn't quite sure what she meant.

Maybe it was that Mo needed sex more often or that she didn't need to be emotionally involved. Mo had sex with a good few different guys in college and before. That was the way it was with most of the young ones. I had this idea of me and her and no one else, even in fantasy. I felt that bond kept us together to the exclusion of all others.

Not that in any way I felt I owned Mo. It was a sharing.

I was going to say something before she left for Spain but I didn't want to hurt her feelings. It wasn't as if we were just casually going out with each other. We were about to become life partners.

Mo loved sex.

She used vibrators while I was watching. It was a huge turn on but I eventually resented the Rampant Rabbits. The constant drone was a pneumatic drill in my head. I was jealous of a machine. She parked the Rabbits in a drawer in her bedside locker. 'The warren,' she called it. Mo told me she would get rid of her collection, if that's what I wanted. Mo found it impossible to get to sleep without some sort of sexual activity.

I gave an okay. 'Better to be counting Rabbits than eating sleeping tablets.'

For my Mo, pre-sleep sex was a bedtime book.

Maureen was Mo's mammy now, but Maureen was more loco than parentis.

She went on a crash grapefruit-only diet and lost two and a half stone in three weeks.

At the end of the grapefruit diet Maureen sucked in her tummy and showed the new waistline to Mo.

'Look at me, Mo, look at me. I'm only two bellies more than regulation.'

Maureen always hated her eyebrows which she said were two hairy caterpillars. The kids in her school used to ask the young Maureen if she was Groucho Marx's daughter.

Maureen booked an appointment at a hair removal clinic.

'They're butterflies now. And they've flown away,' the therapist said.

All that was left over Maureen's eyes were parallel, pencil-thin lines in the shape of upside down half moons. Maureen's hairy legs were reduced to hedgehog stubble by Mo, and she had the beautician smooth her shins with electrolysis and creams. Maureen's big purple lips were

injected with collagen 'for fullness and firmness'. She wore
Marilyn Monroe's lipstick. A new set of long, pointy purple
nails were grafted on to the stumps of the bitten-down
natural ones. Her teeth were whitened and her skin was
browned.

Maureen cut a strip of fabric from her bedspread and
showed it to the hairdresser who Maureen said was 'a small
bit gay, but he was a genius and very nice.' Maureen's furze
hair was tamed and coloured Papal Yellow.

She was made over from top to toe, for the holiday.

Mo didn't tell Maureen about us. I'm sure Maureen
must have suspected when Mo mentioned, pretend casually,
she was moving in to my house 'down the country, for a
little while, until I get sorted.' And she would visit Maureen
'every two or three weeks, at the very least.' Mo softened
the blow further by saying to Maureen that she was the
mammy she never had and once again Maureen told Mo
she was the daughter she never had. There were tears but
no ice cream this time, because of the grapefruit diet.

Maureen never once brought up Mo's leaving the
Compound after that.

I could never figure out how Maureen and Mo could
get over a trauma like the one in the foyer of the hospital
and book a holiday, as if nothing had happened. Conflict
had become part of their daily lives. I, in my own way, was
now part of their story.

They were like school kids. Mo and Maureen were all
excited about going away.

Mo handed me an envelope as she was going in through
the security gate at the airport. A large one with bubbles.

The kind of envelope you would send a book in. Mo wrote a big letter G inside a red heart.

'That's the money I owe you, G. My savings bonds came through. It's the money for the teeth and the phone and the laptop and for a good suit for job interviews. Never let it be said a girl from our place didn't pay her debts. You can tell your mother that. Love you.' We didn't kiss as Maureen was looking at us from a distance.

Then Mo was gone through the departure gates. I never told my mother about the money I gave to Mo.

I opened the envelope in the car. Inside was three grand in fifties.

I had a day around the city trying to shift my social welfare payments down south. My old boss wrote me out a really nice reference. Told me he owed twelve million to the banks and that his house was going under the hammer. I felt sorry for him. He was a good guy who just got a little greedy.

I had my fill of the city and couldn't get out quickly enough. The city was hard work in the wet. The incessant rain had the windscreen wipers opening and closing like a manic book. It was nice to be able to think about stuff that didn't involve life and death and getting killed or wishing people were killed or having your ear eaten bitten off by killer dogs or getting threatened by psychopathic husbands.

But I was missing her already.

I, who nothing ever happened to other than the usual stuff like Dad dying, was now on my own. An actor looking out for a part in his next movie. There was nothing going on. No drama, trauma or shocks. In a way I missed being on the edge but I knew too if I kept on going the way I was it would give me cancer or some stress-related disease when I got older.

I'm sure it was the stress that killed Dad. The stress of living with Mam. Maybe Maureen and Dora would say Mam killed Dad, but I'm sure she never wanted him to die. I just wanted Mo and I to be always really happy and to live together until we were really old.

The plan was Mo and Maureen would hire a car and then drive along the coastal highway to the resort and the hotel whatsit with the African lagoon, the palm trees, and the cool optical illusion infinity pool that looked as if it was washing itself into the sea.

A couple of days passed. I spent the time painting our new room. Mam bought curtains and a duvet and told me she would ask Timmy to be on the lookout for work for Mo. I made sure everything matched.

Mo and Maureen were having a lovely time.

The weather was warm and the hotel was beautiful. Miss you to bits and all that sort of stuff. I was sort of thinking of asking Mo for telephone sex but was sort of a bit shy, but Mo being Mo made the suggestion before I did. Which was grand but I ran out of credit.

I went to O'Brien's shop to buy phone time. I handed in a fifty to Mr O'Brien.

'Hey, G, things are so bad now I'll have to give you a half share in the business instead of your change. I heard your mother's news. You're sound with it?'

Mr O'B was a G on his mother's side and he was always looking out for me, ever since Dad died.

'What news is that, Mr O'B?' I asked.

'Ah never mind,' he said with a flick of his wrists, as if he was passing the mother's news like a football.

'I must be after mixin' her up with someone else.'

She must have been on the radio again, talking about premature ejaculation or vaginitis. She was getting worse. My Mam, that is. I didn't want to hear what it was she came out with this time. I hoped people didn't think Dad had the stuff she was on about. Or me.

I apologised to Mo for the call-up interruptus.

We planned to have telephone sex every night of the holiday. A bedtime story, but I just couldn't get through to her every night.

'Hey, Mo?' I asked about ten days in to the trip. 'Is it a nice place for a honeymoon?' All casual like, because I knew she would love if I asked that way.

'Are you askin?'

This time I didn't hesitate. My mind was made up for good now.

'Yeah. Sound out.'

There was an 'Oh G, oh my God, G!'

Mo gasped yes loads of times. Told me she loved me loads of times. Which I sort of knew she would. Then when she calmed down we got back to our usual way.

'Ah, G, I always thought you'd go down one knee, or even on me.'

That very day I bought an engagement ring with the three grand from the bubble envelope. The jeweller asked the size of my fiancée's fingers. It was the first time I had heard Mo referred to as my fiancée.

'She has fingers like a concert pianist.'

The jeweller spoke, 'Oh my Jesus but you have it very

bad.' I was glad he was a city jeweller and the word wouldn't get out around back home of how it was I made such a corny remark.

'You can bring it back if it's too small,' said the jeweller.

'Sometimes,' he continued, 'people madly in love get measurements all wrong.'

Mo had been in a car accident and was waiting to see a doctor in a hospital near the hotel.

The radiographer diagnosed a dislocated finger. It would have to be reset under local anaesthetic. Mo was very upset and I tried to calm her down.

'That's not so bad. A finger?'

It got worse.

'G, it wasn't my fault. I swear it wasn't. It wasn't really a car crash. More of an accident.'

I took a deep breath. To make sure I was calm and didn't make the situation any worse.

'Were other people injured?' I asked.

'No, just two dogs. Maureen's okay. She's trying to get in touch with the Irish consulate in Las Palmas but the cops took her to the police station. G, I was actually arrested. Can you get on to whatever office deals with Irish people in trouble in Spain?'

Her voice was croaky. I could only just hear her. There

was someone speaking Spanish like as if on a radio in the background.

'There's no need to come down here. It's going to be okay. Stay home. The flights will cost a fortune if you book last minute. Promise me you will stay at home. Promise.'

Then her phone went dead.

It didn't take me long to get a plan together.

I would get on the next flight to Gran Canaria and sort out whatever it was that had happened.

She would do the same for me. This time I would not fail her.

There was no phone coverage.

It could be the Spanish cops confiscated the mobiles. I was pretty sure there was a flight out the next day from somewhere either here or in the UK. My mother took everything in and while I was booking a flight she made a few enquires of her own.

Funny thing was that when I came back in to our lounge she was on Skype to the twins.

'Who switched you on?' I asked.

'Myself,' she replied.

The flights were booked and Mam said if I didn't mind she would call Timmy, and ask him to make enquiries as to what was happening over in Gran Canaria.

'Good idea.'

'Well,' said my mother, ' I partly guessed you'd be alright with that suggestion so I made the phone call to Timmy while you were booking the flights.'

You couldn't be up to her.

By the time I reached the hotel on Gran Canaria, it was nearly ten at night.

The hotel lobby was the size of a football pitch, with chandeliers hanging down off the ceilings like huge costume jewellery earrings.

At the desk I made enquires. Mo and Maureen were staying in a large suite, which must have cost a fortune in a place like this.

There was no reply from their rooms. The mobiles were still powered off.

I didn't really know what to do or where to go at that hour of the night.

I walked by the banks of the African lagoon until I came to a huge thatched area where several hundred people were drinking and dancing to middle of the road covers from an out of tune band singing in bad English accents. Dads twirled small kids and even smaller kids danced short steps and half twirls without a care in the world. I thought it would be a lovely place to go on a family holiday, if we could afford it.

There I was wandering around, dirty, tired and hungry with my bag hanging off my back among the men in shorts and the tall, tanned ladies in the summer dresses and high heels.

When I asked for a water, the waiter muttered something like you have to have a room card, which I clearly didn't have.

By then I was so thirsty I could have taken a drink out of the chlorinated lagoon.

I was making my way to Mo's room, even though there was no reply on the phone, but at least I would be somewhere she might be.

The background set was tall palm trees covered in

hundreds of tiny white lights. The moon was a crescent and a shiny star was attached by an invisible spider thread. And then I thought, in a place like this, it could've been a satellite masquerading as a star.

There were full-sized elephants standing in the lagoon down below and it took a second look to figure they weren't real. I knew my elephants. I was an elephant expert from the time I was a kid. They were Indian, not African. But the island was off the coast of Africa. The statue of the camel had one hump. At least they got that much right.

It was all so touristy, except for the moon and star that is. If it was a star, but it was beautiful and strange to find an African Vegas on a remote rock in the middle of the Atlantic.

I was so thirsty, so worn out. Worried sick. Alone. Didn't have a clue what to do next. I felt too young and inexperienced. Mo was right. Maybe I should have stayed at home. Would she and Maureen think I was crashing their party? What would Maureen's reaction be when she saw her daughter-in-law's new fiancée? But I felt I had to be there for Mo. I swore I would always be there for Mo from now on.

The hotel was playing euthanasia mood music in the corridors.

Distracted, I took a wrong turn – there must have been a thousand rooms in the place – and soon found myself in a bedroom area on a balcony. I looked down from the open stairwell and scanned the floor below.

There was Mo, between the African lagoon and the thatched kraal, with her finger sticking up in a plaster at right angles and her arm in a sling. This guy, a blond-looking big guy, was walking beside her. They didn't notice me as he key-carded the door and she walked into a room behind a huge Roman column. I ran through the corridors and down the stairs to the next level. I couldn't be sure but I figured out it was either room 5643 or 5645. How is it the numbers in hotels are never consecutive?

Was the big man her bedtime story?

I wanted to see the good in her. Trust her. I knew her for nearly six years and surely she wouldn't do this to me. There had to be an explanation. The man might just have been a friend she made on holidays and his wife might have been in the room.

This was the woman with whom I was going to spend the rest of my life. I proposed to her over the phone just a day and a half ago. The jeweller said she was my fiancée. I had an engagement ring in my pocket but the ring finger was dislocated. Was it some sort of Law of the Wish omen? Not that I believed in the Law of the Wish.

By the entrance to the two rooms, just behind the fibreglass Roman column, was a huge rain forest plant with giant fronds. Lying in the middle of one of the leaves like Thumbelina in Dad's stories, was a key card. It was obviously a hiding place for whoever was staying in room 5643 or 5645. Possibly Mo left it out in the frond for Maureen. I could always say I was given the key at reception, but that would be a lie and I didn't tell lies to Mo.

I had to think now. Would I go into the room without knocking? There was no number on the key card. Again I tried Mo's phone. This time there was a dial tone but it stopped after a few seconds.

I entered 5643 with the frond key card and yes there was a couple in bed. An old couple, full of sleep, after a long day in the sun. He was thin and his skinny, almost emaciated arm was wrapped around the old lady. She had long blonde-grey hair and the two were entwined in a soft embrace.

The sliding door of the balcony was open. I tiptoed across the room.

The man stirred ever so slightly in his sleep and took his arm away from his partner who responded by moving closer to him until her shape and his merged into one. I watched and waited for a moment to check if they were sound asleep. And I was sad. Mam and Dad never had this. They used to sleep in different rooms, because she said Dad snored after a few pints.

I walked out onto the balcony which was separated from 5645 by a high green block-work wall. If I stood on the plastic table on the balcony, I would have been able to spy on the next room, which was probably the one Mo and the big blond man walked into just a few minutes earlier.

I was ashamed of myself all over again. For doubting the woman I loved.

I thought I heard a whisper from the old people's room. What it was I couldn't make out. It might even have been the end of a snore or an exhalation. There was the faintest ruffle of a duvet. A wind from the Sahara blew softly through the open patio doors. That might have been enough to wake the old couple, if they weren't awake already. An intruder in their room might give them a terrible shock or a heart attack.

I climbed on the plastic table on the balcony and from

there I managed to scamper up onto the dividing wall.

There, in the shadows of the room, two entangled lovers were making out on the huge bed.

He was on top of her. Mo opened her eyes and saw me on the wall.

I jumped off on the old people's side and ran through the room.

The old lady came out of the bathroom.

She too was naked and hurried to the bed where her husband was now stirring himself.

'I'm very sorry. Wrong room.' I was halfway down the corridor before the door closed.

The running and the shock made me sick. I vomited into a huge urn, the sort of container they used to store grain, in the Old Testament.

The security men were making their way to the old couple's room. I said a Hail Mary for the old people. That they wouldn't get a heart attack. I ran over towards the lagoon, and slipped into the water.

The plaster alligators and white rhinos gave me safe passage. A potbellied pelican with a dust bin beak had a Mars bar wrapper stuck in his lower lip. A flotilla of plastic pink birds with thin legs stood motionless in the middle of the flow, looking up at a winking plane overhead. For a moment I thought this was another dream and I was on the set of a movie.

The security guards scanned the lagoon from a rope bridge. I slipped under the hands-out leaves of a palm tree. The men left the bridge and I dipped my head under the water. Like the dusty ostrich on the far bank, my hidden head would make me the rest of me invisible.

The security men were walking down the banks of the lagoon in between the baobab trees and parallel lines of closed, decommissioned sun umbrellas.

They lifted me out of the water like I was some sort of big fish.

My head was crazy now.

'Are you going to measure me,' I asked 'and throw me back because I'm too small, like they do in the angling on TV? No one eats the fish in them programmes anyway.'

The bigger of the two men put me in an arm lock.

'He on drugs,' said the other.

The police came to the hotel and I was taken into custody. The old people in the room didn't press charges. Mo told them the truth. I signed forms and Mo was waiting for me outside the police HQ.

'I'm so sorry,' she whispered in a sad and tiny voice.

Mo had either a love bite or an insect mark on her neck.

I looked at Mo for a few seconds, not in an angry or a spiteful way. I stared at her coldly as if she was a human experiment. Mo was silent. Her eyes were frightened. Like she was when Dermo was on the warpath.

I think she was hoping I would give out to her and lose my temper. Get it all out in one big blow out and that would be that. But I didn't. I studied her as you would a character in a book, who might come up in an English exam. There was a chasm between us even though she was only two metres from me. Mo looked small now in her sandals and sarong, as if what she did to us diminished her.

I was her best chance. There would have been a proper home with kids. Where, I didn't rightly know but somewhere safe and okay and if something bad happened, it wouldn't be caused by me.

Some inner voice was telling me this was only sex, which was no more than a physical act for Mo. That she was one of generation sex and it was no big deal.

As if echoing my thoughts, and it often happened between us, Mo said, 'It meant nothing to me. It was just physical, a last fling thing. Look I'm some sort of addict I know but I swear on my dead baby. I will never do this to you again.'

I knew what she was saying was true. Knew she wouldn't swear on her little baby unless she meant it. It wasn't the sex act that got to me. This much I made up my mind about in the waters of the lagoon. It was the realisation that this woman whom I loved more than any woman ever and would die for, was beyond hope. Bad stuff would always find her and she would always find bad stuff.

There were no parting words.

I turned and walked away up the road.

Mo followed. Desperately pleading, 'I love you, I love you, G. I'm so sorry. Wait up, G. Please wait up'.

But I couldn't speak. There was no working this out with Mo. There was the shock of it all. The fall from what we had. I broke into a run and she couldn't keep up.

'I'm so sorry, G!' she cried after me in a shriek that seemed to last forever.

The pounding of my feet on the fragile timbers of the ocean boardwalk and the distance I put between us muffled her cries. I could hear the thudding rhythm of my running on the boards. It was as if I was listening to my own heartbeat on a hospital monitor. Slap Bang. Slap Bang. I shut everything else out. Every few seconds there was a whoosh of the incoming waves. Slap Bang Whoosh. Slap bang, slap bang, slap bang, slap bang whoosh. No room in that rhythm for incoming thoughts or listening to Mo.

I counted the waves. The seventh was the deadly wave. It was bigger than the others but it didn't sweep me off and the seventh wave licked the shore like a puppy.

The night diners looked out at me as I ran on, and back at Mo, flapping after me with her flip flops slapping. But I shut it all out. Counted the waves.

The boarded walkway ended at a rocky stretch of shore. I ran up a narrow laneway by a mock Irish Bar with one of those stupid names nobody ever uses back home, like The Liar O'Shea's, or something like that. Past there, I found myself in a street of outdoor bars, restaurants and stalls selling every sort of rubbish.

Three large women bathed their feet in fish tanks with small tiny fish eating away at all the hard flesh on their soles.

I stood on a bench and scanned the street, but there was no sign of Mo.

A red toy insect buzzed above my head. And it hit me. The street vendor apologised and offered me two for the price of one.

The woman who ran the flesh-eating fish stall asked if I wanted a treatment.

My left eye was stinging from the chlorine in the lagoon. There was a chemist sign at the end of the street. I risked going back, parallel to the direction I had been running from. My eye was burning a hole through my head like some sort of creature was trying to burrow inside my brain.

The Irish lady on the plane coming over warned me not to eat any salads in the Canaries.

She told of the young Irish girl, on her honeymoon, who thought the tiny crunchy seeds nestling in her lettuce were linseed pips. They were in fact lizard eggs and they hatched inside her.

The woman told me the young honeymooner was in excruciating pain as the lizards tried to eat their way out through her stomach. She didn't know what was wrong, until the most ambitious and hungry baby lizard stuck his head out through her navel for a peep. Like a kangaroo kid checking the weather in Oz.

Yeah that was the lowest point. There was only one person I wanted desperately to share that with and it was Mo. She would have loved the urban myth. I could imagine her throwing back her head and surrendering her body to the laugh. For over six years all my jokes, all my thoughts, and all my intellectual output was written for Mo.

The chemist gave me drops for the eye.

Mo hurried down the shack street.

Maureen followed, waddling from side to side like an overloaded lorry on a bog road. She was orange, drenched in sweat and out of breath.

I hid in a shop selling sunglasses, swimming trunks, towels, fake Barcelona football jerseys and fridge magnets.

'You like a watch?' asked the salesman.

'Just looking.'

I moved behind a large stand with newspapers from all over Europe.

Between *Der Spiegel* and *The Sun* I could see Mo and Maureen cut into a bar.

The shop assistant asked if I wanted to buy a video camera.

'Special price for you, my friend.'

I could see Mo and Maureen through the peep hole in the canvass wall that separated the shop from the bar.

Mo's eyes were red and swollen. She draped a scarf over the bite.

There were sound bites too, above the humming talk in the cafe, the street noises, the music and the whoosh and splish of the waves.

The sea breeze freshened and I took in huge gulps of air. After a couple of minutes I felt well enough to leave, but I couldn't.

I lay on my front. Mo's painted toes were flicking up and down in the flip-flops with the little strawberry on top, the pair she wore in bed with the big blond guy from Germany or wherever. Possibly he was a Viking, just like her beloved husband.

It was then I heard her piped words travel on the wind through an invisible acoustic tunnel and out under the canvass.

'G is the only the man who was ever nice to me, always.'

There were more words lost in the rising winds that gave power to the waves and the flapping canvass walls of the plastic street.

A cat jumped down from the roof a timber store. I shouted out with the fright. I risked giving away my hiding place. Mo looked up and said something. She got up from her chair. Maureen placed her hands on Mo's shoulders and sat her down. I still couldn't leave her in the state she was in and I began to weaken. But were there others? More lovers? Love wasn't the word for what went on in that room. Pity turned to anger. What was there to say to her anyway?

Whoa babe. How did you enjoy your euroshag?

Was he as good as little G?

Hope you didn't have to wear his crash helmet to stop yourself getting hurt on the headboard of his bed? He being such a big old Viking with his two-horn helmet and him thrusting and bulling and snorting. It was then it dawned on me the Viking was a Dermo lookalike.

I was shaking now. There was a controlling voice telling me not to lower myself to her level. It was an us and them voice. A stick to your own kind voice.

But until I caught her with the pumping piston, where she came from never bothered me. Was I jealous then?

I began to think her bull was laughing at me. Maybe if Mo was a man it would be seen as holiday randiness and a sowing of wild oats in the last laddish victimless sex before marriage.

The conflicting thoughts and emotions swirled around in my brain.

I was so desperately sad then. I knew too that even if I ever met another woman, there would be three of us in the relationship. Mo, her and me.

I desperately needed to be loved and to love back. To be ordinary. Not to stand out for being anything other than a decent guy, who looked after his family and didn't get into trouble, and changed the world in a small way, by just being nice to people.

Words from somewhere fundamentalist came in front of my eyes in bold Gothic 50 font. Words like adultery, fornication and promiscuity.

My mother never used such words. Even before her radio days, she was for sex in certain cases. My Dad told me on the night of our second pint together that I should 'ride all round' me while I was able.

Some biblical prophet from over the water in the Middle East might have taken over my psyche and burned the words into me. I was ashamed to tell Mo at the time. That night in the Compound was my first time. I always promised myself I wouldn't have sex until I met someone I truly loved. That was me and I didn't give in to peer pressure.

So how far do you go? Do you forgive all faults and failings? Can you love someone so much you eventually turn into an enabler like the husband back in our home place, who buys bottles of gin for the wife drinking herself to death behind closed doors?

John Steinbeck, my hero, wrote you have to believe in the perfectibility of man. I'm sure Steinbeck couldn't have known a Mo. She was Mo and if change was to come there would be many events in between the beginning and the final product. Mo was a work in progress that would never be completed. A ghost estate.

The beauty of her haunts me. If I had stayed the sadness of her eyes with the playback of every tough year could have softened me.

No shame came through in her words of apology at the car. Sex for Mo was no more of a physical act than eating an ice cream for pleasure.

Her remorse was not for what she had done but for the effect the act in 5645 had on me.

I had this terrible vision right in front of me. I was

THE BALLAD OF MO & G

pulling Mo from the bubbling waters in front of the boardwalk. Cradling her in a white shift, with her wet hair hanging like seaweed.

Dark empty sockets. A voice from the *Moby-Dick*. A book we did at school. A barnacled Nantucket voice saying knowingly, 'The crabs got her eyes.' Mo, pale and washed out. Anaemic and cold beyond ever warming. It was a horrific wide-awake nightmare and another of those desperate voices crying for attention in the confusion inside my head.

This was my last chance to save her. There can be no doubt but I understood the consequences of leaving Mo to the mercy of the winds, the sea and Maureen Olsen.

I left then. The walk away was fast and furious. In minutes I was on a nudist beach. I threw the engagement ring into the sea. Then I had this terrible, horrible picture of a leathery old pervert harvesting it from the incoming tide.

Into the sea I went, and dived under the water. It was crazy. There wasn't a chance of finding the ring.

I left the sea before the seventh deadly wave.

I made my way home to Ireland the very next day.

Timmy collected me at the airport. He had the full story of Mo's accident.

It seems Mo was driving and Maureen was in the front seat when their jeep hit a poodle. Mo and Maureen jumped from the car. The curly dog was wearing a little tartan waistcoat and a diamond stud collar.

The poodle was squirming around on the hot tarmac like a permed wig, gasping for breath, shaking and quivering and squealing.

Mo ran to a nearby shop for water but in so doing tripped over a piece of concrete that was sticking just above the level.

She put out her hands to stop herself falling but there was no guard rail and Mo banged the finger next to her index finger off a large boulder. The finger was dislocated and Mo ran back in a panic with the piece of paving brick that had become dislodged when she fell. Probably to show Maureen how it was she fell.

Maureen took the brick from Mo and smashed the poodle on the head, killing her instantly. In her statement to the Canarian police, Maureen genuinely thought the dog was in terrible pain and wanted to put her out her misery.

Mo turned around to get away from the spray of blood and poodle brains.

There was another white poodle stuck on to the grill of the hired Pajero.

This poodle was definitely dead.

'Jesus,' Mo asked Maureen, 'did we hit two poodles?'

Maureen was in a state.

'I'm dead certain we only banged into the one.'

By now a crowd had gathered. A woman by the name of Alice Lackabegley from Feakle in County Clare had a good year on the family farm. Her husband Lee sent Alice and her sister Sumatra off on a two-week break in Gran Canaria. Alice videoed the entire incident.

The owner of the mercy killing poodle arrived and Alice showed her an action replay of the cull on the small, square screen of her Sony.

It seems the poodle ran off and the large woman wearing silver high heels who owned it couldn't catch the little dog. The mercy-killed poodle, not used to such freedom, was chasing the escapee in-heat poodle now stuck on the grid of the Pajero like an installation in one of those grizzly art exhibitions of body parts and dead people's organs steeping in formaldehyde.

Not used to exercise and wearing a wooly coat in such searing heat and panting with animal passion, the male poodle was quickly out of breath and dehydrated.

All the male poodle needed was a drink of water. But

Maureen wasn't to know this. She only knew there was a thud when the in-heat poodle was struck down.

The police arrived and Mo and Maureen were taken away in handcuffs.

So it is that an event such as the careless handling of a couple of poodles can change people's lives forever.

Maureen cried so much, the owners of both poodles were won over and the two were released after nearly thirty-six hours in custody.

Maureen paid a thousand euros each to the owners and left the police wondering at why any tourist would carry such money. The police checked out Maureen with their colleagues in Ireland.

Timmy was pretty sure Maureen was not in any way involved but she must have known it was going on, her being a smart woman and all that. Her Dermo was thought to have been up to his eyes in the transportation of the drugs.

Everyone finds everything out about everyone in Ireland, eventually.

Timmy told me I was mixing with a bad lot and it was inevitable I would become a target as these drug gangs had no scruples when it came to killing people. The going rate for a hit was €2,700, down 10 percent due to the rebalancing.

My mother, who wasn't aware of Room 5645, took the liberal view.

'Mo needs our support.' Always welcome and all that, if she was to be my future partner.

Timmy shifted around on his seat, shining the seat of his pants and the chair simultaneously.

My mother wasn't in the least bit bothered while Timmy circled the rim of his tea mug with his index finger.

'Now first and foremost,' said my Mam, 'you know I love you and your brothers and I think on the whole I have been a good mother to you.'

This was unusual in itself in that my mother didn't usually say stuff like 'I love you'. Our house was the opposite to most in that the love stuff was my Dad's job. Mother saw these expressions as meaningless unless backed up with doing stuff like hanging up pictures and cutting the lawn with a scissors or whatever hardships she lined up for him and which he refused to do mainly because he didn't know how and /or he was too lazy.

I always thought my mother would have been happy if she married a handyman.

'About a year ago when I got the hang of that laptop you bought me, I joined a dating agency for the over fifties and it was there I met someone I knew for many years. That someone was Timmy. We are in a serious relationship and Timmy will be moving in here soon. I just wanted to reassure you this will always be your home. Isn't that right, Timmy?

'Yes indeed, Mary,' agreed Timmy, right on cue.

'I'm on your side, Chief.' Timmy looked at me with the sincerity lasering a hole through my head.

I think I was the Chief he was referring to but it might well have been my mother.

I turned on the television. Another soap, just like my life. Some Aussie dickhead with bigger tits than some chick he was shagging was poncing around Summer Bay or somesuch kip, where there's more bother than hell.

My mother looked nervously over at Timmy, who was still circling the rim of his mug. This time Timmy was travelling anti-clockwise, and going so fast I thought he would burn off his fingerprints. There was no way I could explain why I turned on the TV. I turned down the sound. The pictures were enough to blot out my own internal channel.

'Sorry, I suppose I'm a bit nervous. Ah sure no bother. That's okay. Sound.'

My mother told Timmy to stop with the cup.

'I'll be very good to your mother and I know I can never replace your father but I hope we can be friends, Chief.'

If he stopped calling me Chief in that patronising voice of his, I mightn't have minded too much.

I knew immediately that life in our house would never be the same. I wouldn't be able to dump my clothes on the bedroom floor or pick what I wanted for dinner. Timmy would get at the sports pages before me.

My mother was entitled to a partner and in a way it freed me from the duty of looking after her in my role as man of the house. But I knew that from now on, I would be a lodger in my own home.

I left the room with a 'Well that's okay so.' It wasn't a very mature response from me, who was born mature, but I could hardly throw my arms around my new Dad and say 'Hey, I love you man!'

Timmy walked out the door after me.

'By the way, Chief, I signed a pre-nup.'

My mother, who always stuck up for people she loved, other than Dad, added 'And it was Timmy's own idea.'

Time to go, I thought. Time to leave home, for good.

A big man like Timmy was bound to make noise in the bedroom.

A couple of days later I attended a recruitment fair for Oz in the Burlington Hotel. Hundreds queued just to register.

The Aussies promised they would find me a job. My 1:1 and my two years working in the city during the boom gave me as much experience as ten ordinary years and responsibilities well beyond my age.

The money would be okay and I would be with the twins. There would be no fear of the mother. How could you worry about someone who had a policeman kissing her and could fix up her own Skype?

That was how she told the twins. On Skype, with Hubby 2-to-be sitting in the background, like the cat who got the cream.

Timmy looked earnestly into the camera and waved a big wave.

The boys were shocked. They used the word gross a lot and said they knew now why Timmy burst a gut getting them out of that dope rap.

The twins were ecstatic at the thought of my joining them.

'You'll love this one, Chief,' said Al.

'Guess what you're brother shagged last week.'

'It's "who"? Not what, you illiterate git.' I was always correcting them. I made a vow that would stop when I go to Oz.

'He shagged a sheila from Mayo whose name was Sheila but she's had to change it to She-she since she came out here.'

Yeah, Oz was the place for me alright. I never really got that mad, carefree stuff the twins had. I was always the Chief, what with poor old Dad dying young and all that. I'd miss him. Felt almost as if I was deserting Dad. Leaving him alone up in the graveyard, with his hair growing away in his ears.

It was now that I'd love one of his kisses. Lately it's as if his physical presence is fading away. I remember his face alright and his accent but when I go back, the pictures I have of him lack depth, focus and background.

I always imagined Dad was sitting at his usual seat at the kitchen table. It was comforting in a way but now I felt he too was on his way out of our home. I hated leaving him but maybe this was Dad's way of telling me it was time to go. His letting go.

I could always come back in a couple of years. Who knows? By 2015, the country might be back on its feet. I would have a stake. Spare up my money and return like all the emigrants promise to do before they leave home.

But would I be frozen with the cold ? Would it take fifteen years for the economy to get fixed?

The thought of swapping barbie marinade recipes with some plonker named Rip, who surfed and could look on at deadly birds in deadly bikinis without getting an erection sort of put me off Oz. But maybe that was a cliché.

And then when I get there it would be me ringing up my mother and telling her we had Christmas dinner on the beach and her wondering how we cooked the turkey on the strand and how did we boil the ham. Then after five years we would go home on holiday and give out about the weather in Ireland and the lads in the village would say I had an Aussie accent and I would overcompensate by talking like a complete yokel with marbles in his mouth and H's in words like shnow and shteak.

My new Dad's last wife must have died of boredom. Or so the boys in the Baltimore Bar told me. Timmy went on forever with very long stories and trapped people with his bulk in the corner of the local pub so as to make sure they would have to listen to his every word.

We drank all night and talked shite and the lads making out how lucky I was to be heading for Oz and them stuck here on a farm having fantasies over heifers. What with all the young ones gone to Oz and Dublin. But I knew they were just trying to make me feel good. Most of those who left would've stayed here or returned home after a year or two if there was work.

'I'll be back in a year or two with the twins,' I said to Mam.

'They said that in our day,' she replied in a sad and resigned voice, 'but they stayed away. There was nothing here for them in our time either and America wasn't too bad. There were Irish bars and Gaelic football and hurling clubs. Enough to keep you going and a network to back you up that was tighter and more loyal than any group at home, except maybe family.

'There will always be a welcome here for you and the twins. Don't ever forget that.'

There was a knock on the door of my bedroom and then another knock.

I had the Baltimore Bar fear. All sorts of thoughts went through my head. Drink made me depressed.

I just knew I had to get out of Ireland but I was scared of leaving home. Of making a new life in a country where I was a guest, and not a citizen.

Timmy knocked again on the bedroom door. Mam was away in the city for the day. Shopping for her trousseau or whatever it was brides who were round the track before wore on their second big day out.

I pretended to be fast asleep. Thought Timmy was coming in with a tray of sunny-side-up breakfast and that he would want another ages and ages, buddy-daddy chat.

Timmy half-opened the door.

'Hey, Chief we need to talk. It's very important. I'll wait for you in the sitting room.'

'She calls it the lounge,' I replied.

'Chief, it really is serious.' As he turned out the door he looked back and said, 'I have bad news, very bad news.'

I sat up in the bed.

'Tell me now,' I pleaded. 'Is it Mo? Something happened to her?

Mo was the first name that came into my mind in the context of bad news.

The drip-drip of information had something to do with the fact the Gardaí are trained to prepare people for the worst.

Wide awake now.

I pulled on a black top. It was the right colour for what I was about to hear.

'Mo and Maureen have been involved in serious incident at approximately 10.14 am this morning at Mo's residence in a place known as the Olsen Compound.'

Timmy spoke like he was delivering a report on the six o'clock news.

I relaxed. Certain it was something innocuous like blowing up the Dáil or accidentally shooting the President or whatever shit it was they were up to in their world, where people fell off the side into stats every day. The way Timmy spoke in his on-duty cop-talk voice relaxed me a bit.

Timmy sat on the bed.

'Chief, you must be brave now. I have terrible sad news.'

He paused to let it sink in.

Tim took a deep breath.

'Mo . . .' and he stopped. The Garda delivering the report professionally was all but gone now. His voice broke and then he composed himself with another deep breath.

'Mo and Maureen were shot this morning. The news

isn't good. Mo died on her way to hospital and Maureen died at the scene.'

I just lay in the bed as if I too was dead. Laid out, unable to move.

My mother called.

So sorry and was I okay. On her way home. Don't do anything stupid. Drink tea with lots of sugar for the shock.

'Dermo didn't even have the good grace to turn the gun on himself,' said Timmy.

'He's in custody. He shot them with a gun he kept hidden at the house. It seems he snuck out from the hospital. He must have had help.'

I couldn't speak. I tried but no words came out. It was as if I had a stroke or a dentist froze my tongue.

'Chief are you okay?'

I nodded.

'Dermo claimed Mo allegedly borrowed or took money from his stash for a holiday. He shot Mo first and then the mother, who died instantly. Mo died in transit to the hospital. We're not really sure what happened, to be honest. It's too early yet.'

All I could do was keep saying silent Holy Marys to myself in my head but the words were mixed up.

'I'm so sorry, G. But you had a very lucky escape. He was going to get you too.'

I asked Timmy if it wasn't all some sort of terrible mistake. Mistaken identity or could it be she was still alive.

'I wish it was,' he said. 'Sorry, G. So sorry. Old pal.'

'Don't call me old pal!' I shouted. 'Only Dad calls me old pal. And you're not my Dad and you never will be.'

There were no tears. Somehow I knew there would be a

sad story. It was like when you're watching a movie and you know the end right at the start.

Timmy kept calm. He told me there was no point in going to the city and the hospital in my state. I was in shock and he made me tea with lots of sugar. I started to shake. I was gasping for breath like a fish on the river bank. I told Timmy I was getting a heart attack. I couldn't breathe.

The doctor diagnosed a panic attack. He gave me something to calm me.

I slept, woke, slept, woke. It was a waking up from a bad dream, but every time Mo was still dead.

It wasn't as if we lived together properly.

We never even had a whole night in the same bed.

I didn't see her sleeping, her chest heaving ever so slightly like a boat on a calm lake.

Or push back her wispy hair so I could see the beauty of her face. With her eyes closed as she lay on her back, exposed but unafraid in the sanctuary with me. Safe at last. Our toes touching as she woke. And she smiled at me and the new day.

I have difficulty in recalling the next few days.

The papers were full of the murder. Or so I was told. There was some story that Dermo escaped when the police man guarding the hospital skived off to watch *The Sunday Game* in the TV room. Then after a day or two there was no mention of the double homicide. Someone else got shot and the circus moved on.

I stayed in bed for three days, with the curtains drawn, unable to dream, awake or asleep.

At dawn, on the morning of the funeral, I went up the hill to Dad's grave and asked him to look out for Mo.

If there was a heaven, he would surely be there. Dad liked Mo.

Yeah, Dad would mind her for me until my time comes.

Surely by then she would be safe and maybe I would have found my moral and physical courage among the wreckage of a life that for me seemed over before it really got going.

I drove to the funeral.

On my own.

Timmy and Mam begged to go but I needed the peace and isolation of the car. Timmy warned me to watch out for the Olsens but I didn't care if they shot me. It seems they knew about Mo and me. Maureen must have told them when she came back from the holidays.

There was a mass. People went up to the front pews when it was over, to shake hands with a dried-out old woman.

The old lady sat in the front seat, on her own.

Four or five hundred people packed the church.

Mostly murder-tourists, neighbours, the girl from the nightclub on the first night, old praying people, and journalists.

I could feel the life leaving me. As if I was leaking and didn't really care.

There was communion. I took the host for Mo. Prayed more Hail Marys for her.

Passed by the coffin on the way down. Touched the polished timber.

The priest was making out death wasn't so bad after all. Made a lovely speech. A generic one for one of the many murder victims in Mo's parish.

Mo was alone in her coffin at centre stage in front of the altar, an offering.

All that girl ever wanted was her own home. A little plot, and soon enough at least one wish would be granted.

I joined the cue of hundreds of people at the end. Most of them didn't know Mo.

The old lady took my hand. It was as limp as if she was dead herself.

I didn't have to ask who she was. The old lady was Mo's mammy. I knew her from Mo.

She was pretty once. But there would be no presents now from Bob's pals. I could see from her sunken, broken, forlorn, forsaken, baggy, wrinkled, unreflective eyes Mo's mother knew, she too had failed Mo.

The graveyard I couldn't do. The lowering of her coffin and the thud of the earth on the timber was an erratic last-post drumbeat I never forgot when Dad was buried.

The world went by.

Life was turning tricks.

You expect everything to stop just because you can't go on.

People were making their way to cars with bags of shopping.

An earnest girl with her hair tied up jogged past and a crow stuck his beak in a dunce's cap of popcorn.

A pregnant woman with the pink hair drove a pram while talking on her mobile.

Three old boys were smoking and shifting from foot to foot outside the bookies.

I drove away from it all.

Longing for the isolation.

The car was moving from side to side almost involuntarily.

I didn't really care what happened to me but what if I killed an innocent person?

I asked Dad to help and I was better then.

In the distance was the outline of the Compound.

The police wouldn't let me into the house.

It's a crime scene they said. The perimeter was marked

off with yellow tape. Mo's bloody long fingers were painted on the cream-coloured front wall like ancient cave art.

The detective checked my car reg. Knew who I was.

The Chinese bells tinkled.

The Compound was a scene from an old movie. A set where so much action took place. And now it's The End.

'You were her friend.'

'I was her friend.'

He lit up a cigarette and asked if I'd like one.

'How did she die?' I asked impatiently, while the detective was in the middle of a deep drag. 'Timmy told me but can you show me what happened and where?'

The detective nodded.

He pointed to the bloody porch.

'That's where they died.'

'Can I go in?'

'Better not,' he said. 'There's still forensic work going on.'

But he did tell what happened on the day of the shooting.

'He, the husband, pretended he was much worse. He was able to walk and his injuries were improving. And then one day when security became too relaxed, he escaped. You know the rest.'

The detective looked over my head as if to say there's your way home. But I didn't know the rest. Knowing was better than imagining. For me, who had awake dreams worse than any reality.

I had to know and I told the detective.

'I don't really know the details. You see there are these pictures, in my head, and I can't stop them. I'd like to know and then the pictures might stop.'

The detective thought for a second and then he broke the rules.

'He came here to where he had money stashed, probably from drugs. In a room he called the Den.

'Your friend Mo borrowed or took money thinking he, the husband, would never need it, because he wasn't okay in the head. She produced a marriage cert and ID at the hospital. Took his keys, saying her stuff was locked up in the family home and she couldn't get at it.

'They went on a holiday the next day. The mother and herself. To the sun. But sure you knew that.'

I nodded.

'The bastard waited in the house until she came home. Or that's our guess. He greatly resented the fact that the wife was on holiday spending his money while he was banged up.

'The mother, it seems, from our investigations, threw herself between Mo and the gun. He, the husband was saying he didn't mean to kill his mammy. I have it here.' The policeman walked to his car and came back with a file.

He read in a voice different to his speaking voice. The detective was giving evidence.

'"I wasn't out to kill my mammy. I swear on my father above in St Sepulchre's. My mother thrun herself all of a sudden like in front of that robbin bitch what's a thief and a whore."

'That's all we got out of him. But it's enough to put him away for a long, long time.

'Forensics and the post-mortem backed up his story. The bullet went straight through his own mother, killing her instantly and the same shot wounded Mo.

'He just left her there to die. Mo might have been saved if he dialled 999. She lost so much blood before the ambulance came.'

The kind policeman stopped as if to gather his thoughts.

He looked at me. Eyes full of empathy, as he flicked through the pages of the bound file. 'There's a conversation that took place in the ambulance. Your friend was calling for G as she died. You are G. Your nickname.'

'That's me. She . . . Mo . . . was my . . . my fiancée.'

'I'm so sorry.'

The long silence following the posthumous announcement of the engagement was interrupted by the gunshot sound of a crow scarer. The policeman jumped around and took a gun from a holster inside his jacket.

'It's only the farmers trying to scare away the birds,' I explained.

The embarrassed detective put the gun back in the holster as a clatter of starlings rose up as one from a stubble field a few hundred metres to the east.

'At least we have him now. Crashed his car at those Bad Bends on the road to the motorway. But I'm sure Timmy told you all that.'

I thanked the detective and turned to walk away.

'There's more.

'He's in the Central Criminal Mental Hospital. In Dundrum.

'Rocking and swaying. All day. Just going back and forth. I was almost seasick and hypnotised at the same time from watching him.'

He walked beside me to the car.

'The sign is gone,' I said, pointing to the steel pole where 'Bewear of Dermo' had been tied on with bailer twine. There was never a truer sign.

'Evidence,' said the detective.

'Is there anything else?' I asked. 'Please don't spare me. It's worse not knowing.'

'No, that's it. Although there is one theory, but we can't prove it.

'It seems the mother pretty much wanted reconciliation between Mo and the husband before he was sent down for killing the nun. At least we think that's what happened. There's no way of proving it but she might have helped him to escape.'

'That would be Maureen alright,' I replied.

The cop put an arm round my shoulder as we walked. I stopped to take deep breaths. Almost hyperventilating. He handed me his card.

'I'll be finished here in an hour if you need company.'

I thanked him but said I would be okay. There was somewhere I needed to be. I was driving away when the detective beckoned at me to press down the window button.

'I've been married for nearly twenty-three years and I'll bet I didn't have as many happy days as you and your fiancée.'

I made my way there around dusk. Through the many-graved cemetery in the foothills of the mountains. Past the teddy bears at the kids' plots. Along the flower-strewn narrow streets of the city of the dead. Searching for freshly dug graves. Searching for Mo.

Eventually I found the spot where she was buried. Just one more uneven, rough-seamed jigsaw quilt where the joins in the grass sods were still showing.

Her name was typed on a little strip of tape attached to a knee-high, unvarnished wooden cross.

The graveyard was empty of alive people, bar me.

Darkness fell and we were alone at last

I tried to pray. To talk to her but I felt I had to get nearer. To lie with Mo, for one last time.

The grass scraws were muddy and wet.

I lay down and smelled the earth. It was warm and moist. I could hear the growing, felt the eternal in the scent of the grass, the feeling of life and renewal in a place where there was so much death. There was an energy travelling along and up through the palms of my hands and through my finger tips.

I spoke to my Mo. Told her there was nothing to forgive or if she felt there was then I forgave her.

My good interview suit was covered with mud and my face was muddy too.

Couldn't get up or go. The night fell and it was colder then. Rain came and went in flurries and fits.

Tears too.

The grass stopped growing.

I could hear a slight vibration in the earth and then a-thud a-thud, thud as if an army was bearing down on me.

I looked up and there standing over me was Mikey Olsen. With him was a group of about ten men and a couple of women. I knew from the look of them, they too were Olsens.

This is it now.

The day that you die.

I didn't care.

Mikey bent over and lifted me up.

'Come on now. Don't be afraid of nottin.

'Mo's mammy ordered it that no Olsens would come to the funeral. We're only here to pay our respects.

'Come on now. Your good suit is all dirty.'

We stood silently as the Olsens prayed.

When they finished Mikey called me to one side.

'Do you see that grave what's been dug up over there?'

'Where, Mikey?'

'There, next to where you're standin, 'ahind you.'

'I see it, Mikey.'

'We're puttin' the mother in there tomorrow.'

He helped me to my car. I was stiff and cold as any corpse in the cemetery.

Old Grey snuggled up beside me, rubbing his coat along my leg as I walked, as if in sympathy.

'Don't go blamin' yourself for nottin,' comforted Mikey. 'Poor Mo was a great little girl but she had no luck.'

Mo had no luck. From the day she was born.

The Bad Bends near my own home were almost upon me. Visibility was poor. Fog came in from the sea and there were no gaps in the persistent drizzle.

The car drove itself on autopilot.

I lost concentration. There was a swerve and the car skirted the ditch. The wing mirror was broken off. I drove on but the images were in front of me.

204

I could see myself standing alone and naked with my hands covering my modesty on a windswept beach, waiting for the two-storey-high house tide to come in.

She smiled at me. Knew me in that smile. Knowing, and accepting and understanding the last verse of the Ballad of Mo and G.

Then it was I knew I could live with myself and bear witness to my own company.

For who was I anyway but young G.

Mo knew her G.

And she knew he wasn't a brave lad but he loved her once and now again, forever.

She could kill me now, if that was her last wish. But she didn't.

Now Oz will take me in. The twins will mind me under each wing as I had done with them.

Mam and Timmy were good.

They drove me to the airport. He, in his attempt to show he understood, tried to hug me but it was awkward because I wasn't capable of any intimacy since Mo died.

Mam cried. Said she loved me.

Tim put his arm around Mam and walked her slowly from the departure area, heads low, home-from-a-funeral gait. They didn't look back. I ran to them and kissed Mam and hugged Timmy.

The Ballad of Mo and G has the compulsory sad verse common to all Irish songs of emigration. The one where the boy's sweetheart dies and he goes over the water into exile.

I closed my eyes before the plane took off.

Mo would be the last person I would see before I left Ireland.

There was never any danger when I lost control at the Bad Bends.

For Mo would never kill me.